# MR. ARROGANT

The Keith Brothers
Book 2

## PEYTON BANKS

"You didn't tell me he was coming." Sofie Carter sniffed. She hefted her purse up on her shoulder while walking alongside her best friend, Alana Keith. Her arch nemesis strolled ahead of them conversing with his identical twin brother. How could her friend not tell her that he was going to be there? She felt slightly betrayed due to the lack of information.

Jaxon Keith had been a thorn in her side from the moment Alana and London had got married. The man lived to get on her nerves. She tried to stay away from him, but that would be impossible if she wanted to continue her friendship with her bestie.

"If I had, you probably would have come up with an excuse not to come with me." Alana laughed.

She rested a hand on the baby she had strapped in a carrier on her chest. The six-month-old lifted his head slightly and glanced over at Sofie. Her heart softened at the sight of her godson. Chance Keith was a beautiful baby who not only had his parents wrapped around his little finger, but her as well.

"Plus, how could you not know," Alana said. "This is a big night for PSM. Jaxon is co-owner with London."

Sofie blew out a deep breath. She knew she was being juvenile and should act like the thirty-three-year-old adult she was, but there was something about Jaxon that rubbed her the wrong way. Maybe it was his arrogance, or the way he thought he was God's gift to women. Even that smirk of his had her wanting to choose violence and punch him in the face.

"Do I have to sit near him?" Sofie asked.

They followed the guys into the Cleveland sports arena. She nodded to the gentleman holding the door open for them. Tonight, the city's basketball team was playing game seven of the championship finals. If they won tonight, they would be league champions. Sofie had spent enough time in the Keith household to pick up on the ins and outs of the sports management business.

"We are in the clubhouse. There will be plenty of room for you to move around, and no, you won't have to sit next to him." Alana laughed. Her eyes sparkled behind her leopard-print frames. She reached over and took Sofie's hand. She gave it a big squeeze before letting go. "I'm just glad that you took off of work to go on the trip with us."

"You think I'm going to pass up an all-expenses-paid trip to Bora Bora? Girl, you would be out of your mind. There is nothing that man could do to make me pass up on this trip." Sofie barked a hefty laugh. She was officially on a two-week vacation from her job at Cleveland General Hospital. As a registered nurse, she had been working crazy hours for a while now, and this was her first real vacation in about two years.

She at first stressed about paying for her part of the trip, but London wouldn't hear of it. She didn't have to be told twice to keep her money. Her bestie's husband was loaded, and if he wanted to make his wife happy by including her best friend in their vacation, who was she to deny him the pleasure of her company?

"I don't know why you don't quit your job and come work with me," Alana said.

They strolled down a hall that led to an elevator. Sofie could already feel the tension and electricity in the atmosphere. It had been a while since Cleveland had won a championship.

This was one thing Sofie loved about her town. The fans of all the sports teams were diehard followers. It didn't matter how bad the team was, Cleveland was going to show up and support. With the basketball team in the finals, the city was on edge.

They passed by quite a few media people who Sofie was sure were covering the game.

"You girls can walk a little faster." Jaxon snickered. He stood in the doorway of an elevator and waited for them.

Sofie narrowed her gaze on him. His infamous smirk grew wider into a full-fledged grin.

"Bite me," Sofie snapped. She joined Alana in the elevator and moved to stand in the back corner away from him.

Alana automatically went to London's side and

slid up under his arm. They made the perfect couple.

"If you want me to." Jaxon shrugged and stepped into the car. The doors slid shut behind him. He threw her a wink before turning to the elevator attendant in the corner. "James, my man. How's the family?"

Sofie hadn't caught sight of the older man whose sole job was to manage the elevators. She never got over that the arena employed someone to do this. She knew it had to do with the area they were in. There were plenty of wealthy people who used these back elevators that went up to the skyboxes, and this must be a part of the luxury price tag for enjoying the game.

Hell, she couldn't believe she was even in this part of the arena. Sofie was a big basketball fan and tried to come to at least a few games a year, but normally her seats would be in the nosebleed sections.

"Everyone is doing fine, Mr. Keith. We're all praying for this championship tonight." The older man chuckled. He was dressed in dark clothing with a sports coat. His stark white hair was combed back away from his face. He was a jolly old man who was pleasant and worked this elevator the few times Sofie had come with the Keiths.

"Aren't we all." Jaxon slapped the man on the shoulder.

"What were you two talking about so intently?" London asked Alana.

Her friend had the audacity to roll her eyes.

"Oh, you know. Me trying to convince her to quit her job so she could come work with me," Alana said.

"It's just not that easy," Sofie said.

Alana had left her job after her maternity leave and opened her own consulting firm. She was hounding Sofie to come work with her. She was desperate to have a medical professional such as Sofie who would be able to review medical claims. It was tempting and would be a big step.

"It is. If you need help writing your resignation letter, I'll help you," Alana offered.

Chance took that opportunity to put in his two cents and squealed. It would appear he agreed with his mother.

"We'll talk about this later," Sofie murmured. Tonight was not the night she would make a decision that would impact her entire life. Nursing had been her career from the moment she'd graduated from college. But lately, she was burned out. It wasn't as fun as it was when she'd first entered the work force.

She was tired of being degraded by patients, yelled at by physicians, made to work with unsafe ratios while no one cared. She loved caring for people, but there had to be a line drawn somewhere. It was already bad that nurses were leaving the field in droves. She just wasn't a quitter, and what Alana offered her was a good deal. She had to really think about it and if it would be a right move for her.

The door opened to the elevator, and Sofie followed London and Alana out. She caught sight of Jaxon slipping James a tip on his way out. The man could be an asshole, but every so often she'd catch him doing something that was out of character for him.

She didn't know how, but somehow Jaxon arrived beside her, strolling down the curved hall toward the skybox he and his brother had bought out. She scowled, shooting daggers at the back of her friend's head. She tried to increase her pace, but his long legs allowed him to easily keep pace with her.

"I hear you're coming with us to Bora Bora," Jaxon's deep voice broke through the silence.

She sighed and sent up a prayer. She eyed him and cursed internally when her heart skipped a beat.

Why did he have to be so damn handsome? With his dark hair, stormy-gray eyes, and perfect physique. Woman clamored to him like flies on shit. She saw the appeal in him but swore she wouldn't give in to her carnal thoughts.

Alana constantly teased her that they didn't get along because of the sexual tension between them. Sofie still couldn't believe Alana had suggested she go ahead and sleep with Jaxon. Her friend was completely dickmatized and apparently wasn't thinking too straight.

She and Jaxon?

No way in hell.

"I am and I hear the place is big enough where I won't have to see you if I don't want to," she replied haughtily.

Jaxon chuckled and elbowed her slightly. She ignored the warm sensation from his skin brushing against hers. A shiver rippled down her spine.

"I'm not that bad."

"To who?" she scoffed.

They had arrived at their destination. London held the door open to allow Alana and Sofie to enter. The guys followed in behind them. There were already other people inside the box. Sofie recognized a few of the sports agents who worked for London and Jaxon along with their guests. They had everything they would need in this room. There was a bar, tables lined up with food being served buffet style. A couple of waiters milled around, ensuring everyone had what they needed. There were two rows of seats in front of the opening that showcased the court down below.

Loud music blared from the speakers. Sofie rushed over to the window so she could look down below and put some distance between her and Jaxon. She took in the scene and grew excited. The atmosphere in the arena was electric. The dance troupe was entertaining the growing crowd. She loved the DJ and the troupe. They knew how to entertain.

"Hey," she called out, swaying to the beat of the music. It was one of the popular songs that was out, and she loved it. The fans were getting involved, clapping and dancing along as well. Other members of the troupe raced around, shooting balled-up t-shirts up from their small handheld canons.

She had a good feeling about tonight. She loved the Cleveland Knights and was a big fan. She sent up a small prayer that her team would secure their victory and championship tonight.

"Oh, look at all the people," Alana murmured. She came to stand beside Sofie. "The game doesn't start for another hour."

"Girl, you do realize this is the championships, right? And, might I add, history that everyone wants to be a part of." Sofie laughed. Her friend wasn't too into sports and wouldn't understand the significance of a team and the final championship game. "And we are going to win tonight. I feel it in my bones."

"I sure do hope so." A newcomer came to stand on the other side of Sofie. He was a nice-looking guy, tall, brown hair with a wide grin. One dimple appeared on one of his cheeks. He was dressed in a white button-down and jeans.

"Sofie, this is Aston. He's an agent for Prime-time. Aston, this is my best friend, Sofie," Alana introduced them.

Sofie took his hand in a warm shake.

"How are you?" she murmured. If all the sports

agents looked like him, maybe she would ask London if they were hiring nurses. Someone had to assess employees or athletes to make sure they were in good health.

"I'm good. You're into basketball?" Aston asked. He sidled closer to Sofie.

She smiled, ignoring her friend's chuckle. Aston was cute, and it would be nice to have someone of the male species pay her attention and not get on her nerves.

"I am and I'm from Cleveland. We always support our teams," she teased.

He barked a laugh and jerked his head in a nod. "I'm learning that. I'm from Chicago, and we're the same way about our teams."

Sofie leaned against the short wall in front of them, giving him her attention. She caught sight of Alana walking over to London from the corner of her eye.

"Chicago, huh? What brought you to Cleveland?" she asked.

"Primetime. I've worked for other agencies, and when the opportunity came to join this company, I practically sold my soul to work for the Keiths. They are awesome to work for." He smiled, and that little dimple revealed itself. He cleared his throat and glanced over at the bar. "Want a drink?"

"I'll take a bourbon," an annoying voice replied from behind Sofie.

She bit back a scowl, sensing Jaxon's eyes on her. She stiffened at how close he was standing behind her.

"Oh, sure, Jaxon. Sofie?" Aston glanced back at her.

"A cranberry and vodka." She offered him a small smile.

He pushed off the wall and walked away. Sofie spun on her heels to face Jaxon.

"What are you doing?" she asked, resting her hands on her waist.

"He offered to get drinks." Jaxon shrugged nonchalantly. He narrowed his eyes on her and stepped closer. "What do you think you are doing?"

"Not that it's any of your business, but I was just having a friendly conversation with another human being."

"Who is my employee."

"And from the looks of it a whole grown-ass man," she snarled.

Jaxon smirked, and her rage rose even higher. What was it about this man that had her acting not like herself? She usually wasn't this aggressive or rage-driven. She was normally a laid-back girl who went with the flow, but when Jaxon came around, everything changed. It was like he pushed all of her buttons to drive her insane.

"And you shouldn't be fraternizing with men who work for me."

"But I don't work for you, and your men can do as they damn well please." She folded her arms in front of her. She arched an eyebrow at him, daring him to say something else.

"You're the best friend of his employer's wife." Jaxon lowered his voice. He erased what little room was between them.

She ignored the warmth that radiated from him, and the scent of his cologne and how she could feel his hardest muscles through his clothes. She took a step back from him. She needed to have some space between them.

The man had the nerve to smirk again as if he knew what she was doing.

"You, Jaxon Keith, are reaching. Why do you care?"

His eyes darkened at her response. He looked away from her and out into the stadium. A muscle in his jaw ticked.

"Here we go," Aston announced, returning with a small tray holding their glasses.

"Thanks, Aston." Sofie smiled widely. She turned away from Jaxon and took her glass.

Aston held the tray out for Jaxon to snag his before he took his off the tray. He set it down on a nearby table, turning back to her.

"To the Knights." Ashton held his glass up for a toast.

"The Knights," Sofie murmured, clinking her glass softly against his.

Apparently, Jaxon didn't take the hint that he wasn't wanted. He pressed to her back and reached out, adding his glass with theirs.

"The Knights." His warm breath blew against her cheek.

A shiver flounced through Sofie at his closeness. She moved away again. She didn't know what game Jaxon was playing.

What he jealous?

There was no way.

He didn't think of her in that way. He was like London before he'd met Alana. The two of them had been man whores. Before Alana had become involved with London, the two of them had watched the parade of women in and out of

London's apartment. The girls had nicknamed him Mr. Hotness.

A woman would have to be blind, deaf, mute, and dumb to not think the Keith brothers were attractive. They turned the heads of any females, and even some males, when they walked by.

She hated to admit how sexy she thought Jaxon was. She didn't want to know of how many women he had been with. She was surprised he hadn't brought a bimbo as a date tonight.

Jaxon without a female companion was a rarity.

If he was bored, then it wasn't Sofie's problem. She turned back to Aston and offered him a smile. She would ignore Jaxon. He could go bother someone else. He was not going to ruin her night.

"So, Aston. Tell me about what you do at Primetime."

Jaxon Keith didn't chase women. He was a man who had women tripping over their feet to get his attention. He never had to be alone if he didn't want to. One thing he couldn't understand was this fascination with Sofie Carter.

Sofie was his brother's wife's best friend. They were around each other a lot, and anytime they were around each other, they argued. There was something about her fiery nature that drew her to him. He couldn't help the words that always flowed from his lips.

This wasn't naturally him.

Jaxon had a way with words, and everyone always liked him. It helped with the business he was in. He had to get well-paid athletes to trust him with their careers and take them to a higher level.

Jaxon had once been one of them. Right after college he was drafted to play professional baseball. He had been one of London's first clients. They had built Primetime Sports Management from the ground up. Jaxon had done everything he could to help PSM while he was playing. He recommended many sports figures to speak with London and the agents.

Jaxon was proud of his older brother. London had worked tirelessly for him when he was playing ball. He'd secured Jaxon endorsements that still brought him hefty checks to this day. After Jaxon's injury, London had welcomed him among the ranks of agents and as part owner.

He might have been a major baseball league player, but he was a businessman at heart. His parents, Larry and Donna Keith, hadn't raised dummies. His mother had always wanted him to have a backup should baseball not work out. Jaxon had listened, and that woman had been right. He would need to fall back on plan B.

He'd blown out his knee. After multiple surgeries and stints of physical rehab, his knee never fully recovered. A few years in the league, he'd had to hang up his bat and gloves.

But his family didn't let him fall into a stupor when he'd retired. His dreams of reaching the professional level had been accomplished, but the man upstairs had other plans for him. His family was there to support him, and by the time he had recovered from his career-ending injury, London had already had his office outfitted for him.

Jaxon's gaze sought out Sofie once again. As much as he tried to ignore her, he found himself staring at her. Her dark hair framed her face, and those almond-shaped eyes and brown orbs always narrowed when they landed on him. She had high, full breasts that he ached to see. What color were her areolas? Would her mounds fill his large hands? Her waist tapered into full hips that flared out, and her ass was one he was sure he would have to thank the good Lord above for if he ever had the chance to sink his teeth into it.

His cock stiffened at the thought of her laid out on a bed, naked, waiting to take his cock.

What. The. Fuck.

The woman couldn't stand him.

He knocked back his drink and slammed the empty glass on the bar.

"Would you like another one, sir?" the bartender asked. He immediately swiped the glass from the counter and began washing it.

"Nah, I'm good." Jaxon turned and leaned against the bar. He was unable to tear his gaze from Sofie and Aston. The two had grown cozy during the game. He bit back a snarl at the thought of Aston making moves on her.

Not that Jaxon had any rights to her. He didn't understand this ache in his chest when he thought of her going out with Aston, or Aston getting a taste of what Jaxon himself wanted.

"If you stare any harder at her, she may come over here and punch you in the face." London slid onto the stool next to him.

"Not sure what you are talking about." Jaxon grunted.

He looked over at his twin. The Keith brothers were identical. There were slight differences between them that only a few people could make out. When they were kids, they had done everything together, dressed the same and even played the same sports.

Women loved identical twins, and the boys had

taken full advantage of it. London was his elder brother by two minutes. They were as close as brothers could be.

"Why are you hesitating on asking her out?" London lowered his voice. His attention was on his wife who was off in the corner with their child. She had a blanket over her chest hiding little Chance. She must be feeding the baby.

"Hesitate? Who said I wanted to take her out?" Jaxon asked.

"Really? You're going to lie to me? I know you better than you do."

"Do not," Jaxon scoffed.

London glanced at him with a raised eyebrow. Jaxon guessed he could admit that no one knew him like his brother. When growing up, there had been plenty of instances where they would be able to hold entire conversations and not even utter one word.

"And you are slipping, big brother. Not sure if you realized it, but me and her don't get along."

"Only because you're an ass to her half the time."

"And you and Alana were smooth sailing when you first met?"

"Um, yeah." London leveled him with a steady look.

Jaxon blew out a deep breath and remembered the first time he had met Alana. She and Sofie had come over to London's apartment searching for him. London had moved out to the house in the suburbs while Jaxon had taken over the downtown condo.

Jaxon was happy for London. He had immediately changed for Alana. No longer was he partying with endless women. It was as if he had matured and grown up. Alana was good for him. London doted on her as if she were his entire world.

Jaxon didn't know anything about that. He loved to have his fun and never saw himself settling down with just one person. If he did, that person would have to be one hell of a woman to rein him in.

His gaze sought out Sofie.

"What's the worse she could say? No?" London murmured.

"Listen, bro. This is one time you don't have me figured out. I'm not interested in her."

He pushed off the bar and moved to the seats. London was determined to try to figure out what was between him and Sofie. It was nothing. For all he knew, this attraction he had for her was because she didn't return the same feelings. His ego was a little damaged by the way she could just ignore him.

He'd get over it. There were plenty of women out there he could choose from. They were about to leave to go to a tropical island for vacation. He was sure he could find a bit of feminine company to keep him busy.

He sat in the back row and settled his attention on the game. The Cleveland Knights were up ten points, and he had a good feeling they were going to take the game.

Khalil Roads, their star, stole the ball from the other team and exploded, running down the court at full speed. The crowd went wild. Jaxon jumped to his feet along with everyone else. The roar in the arena was deafening. Khalil bounced the ball as he ran, his focus on the basket. At the free-throw line, he shot up in the air and slam-dunked the ball in the basket.

Jaxon joined everyone in cheering and yelling. He turned to Brad, one of their senior agents, and high fived him. Jaxon grinned, clapping. The other team called a time out, and the arena went crazy.

Khalil was the biggest superstar in the national basketball league. London had pursued Khalil to sign with PSM. Apparently, with the help of Alana, his brother was able to sign Khalil to their sports agency. London worked really closely with the basketball superstar. Not only had London helped Khalil with receiving one of the largest contracts in the national basketball league history, but the endorsement deals were out of this world.

After signing Khalil, their business had increased threefold. They were already one of the best-known agencies out there, but now everyone wanted them to represent them. They had hired more staff, and Jaxon worked between their two offices, Cleveland and Los Angeles.

"He is a god." Brad laughed. He slapped Jaxon on the back.

"That he is," Jaxon agreed. Khalil was one of those players who was one in a million. He would have a long, prosperous career. "Glad he's signed to us."

He saw movement out of the corner of his eye. He glanced over. Sofie and Aston also stood. Her face was lit up with excitement. He couldn't hear what she was saying, but her hands were moving around erratically as she spoke. But that wasn't what he was staring at.

It was the hand that Aston had resting on the small of her back.

The urge to go over there and rip his arm off exploded inside Jaxon. He blinked and took a few deep breaths. He ran a trembling hand along his face.

*She's not yours*, he had to tell himself.

Going over and trying to warn her off of his employee had been a dick move. He didn't know what had come over him. He just knew he hadn't wanted her smiling at another man.

*She's not yours*, he repeated to himself. This was a new territory for him, and he didn't want to explore it.

The game continued on, and tensions were running high. The opposing team was not going down without a fight. Jaxon couldn't sit down. The thrill of a win was coursing through his veins. He remembered how it felt being the center of attention, having thousands of fans screaming his name. Pushing all thoughts of Sofie aside, he focused on the game before him.

---

"Champagne," Jaxon called out to the flight attendant. He slid into his comfortable seat on the private jet. He offered his fist to London as he passed with Alana and the baby in tow. The Knights had won the championship. This meant a lot for Primetime. As the agency who worked with the biggest basketball star on the planet, they were due to make a lot of money.

"Yes, Mr. Keith," the flight attendant replied. She gave a short nod, spinning around and heading to the front of the small plane.

Jaxon rotated his recliner around and gazed out the window.

He knew without looking the moment Sofie boarded the plane. She took the leather recliner across from Jaxon. Her husky laugh filled the air, and he had to keep himself from turning to stare at her.

"That was an amazing game," she announced.

"It was," Alana agreed.

"You sure you were paying attention? Seemed like you and Aston were getting real cozy." Jaxon slowly swiveled his chair around and met her heated gaze.

"As I told you earlier, that's none of your business," she replied haughtily. She swirled her chair to face Alana who was in the process of handing Chance over to London.

"So you and Aston hit it off?" Alana asked. She took her seat near Sofie and strapped herself in.

"We did. We exchanged numbers," Sofie said.

A deep pain surged inside Jaxon's mouth. He blinked, not realizing he was grinding his teeth. He fought to relax himself.

"Here you go, Mr. Keith."

He glanced up and took in the flight attendant standing next to him with the champagne he had asked for. Her badge held her name, Susan.

"Thank you, Susan. Please ensure everyone has a glass."

"Except me," Alana replied with a small smile.

He glanced at Susan.

"Can I have something non-alcoholic?" Alana requested.

"You can't even have one glass to celebrate?" Jaxon asked. He knew nothing of lactating women. He didn't see how one glass could hurt. Tonight's win for Khalil was a game-changer for them.

"I mean, I could. One glass of wine wouldn't hurt, but I'd rather save that for when London and I are in the hotel tonight for our private celebration." Her face softened as she glanced over at his brother. She pushed her glasses up onto the bridge of her nose.

London tossed her a wink.

"Well, if she doesn't want one, I'll take my glass and hers." Sofie laughed.

"Yes, ma'am." Susan chuckled. She turned her attention to London. "And you, sir. Will you be having champagne?"

"Yes, I will. Just bring my wife a juice, please," London said.

"Yes, sir. I'll be right back. In the meantime, please make sure your seat belts are fastened. We will be taking off soon." She spun on her heel and walked toward the front of the aircraft.

The other attendant closed the door to the plane and disappeared in the front.

Jaxon and his brother had purchased this aircraft a few years ago. He used it often with him flying back and forth from Cleveland and LA. They also used the jet when flying around the country to meet with potential or current clients.

It wasn't long before everyone had their drinks and the plane was off into the air. Jaxon turned around and held his glass up.

"I'd like to make a toast," he began.

Everyone raised their glasses.

He grinned and blew out a deep breath. "To London. You are an amazing man, brother, father, and husband. Without you, none of us would be sitting here on a private jet, flying off to Bora Bora. I've always teased you about your work ethic, but I know it was so we could be a successful company and family. I just want to say I love you and hope to be half the man you are."

"Hear, hear," the girls echoed and sipped their drinks.

"Not necessary. You would have done the same thing had the tables been turned." London chuckled. He sipped his champagne then motioned his glass to Jaxon. "For a little brother, you've been a pain in the ass, but I wouldn't go into business with anyone but you."

"Oh, and to Alana." Jaxon nodded to his sister-in-law. "I hear it was you who truly convinced Khalil to sign to PSM. We are celebrating you for helping take our business to the next elevation."

"I didn't do anything special," Alana grumbled. She pushed her glasses up again. She glanced around the aircraft at them, a smile spreading. "But if y'all need help again, just let me know."

They all fell into a fit of laughter. Susan came around and ensured their glasses were refilled.

Jaxon sat back and eyed Sofie. She rolled her eyes at him and spun her chair to face Alana.

"One more thing," Jaxon announced.

He raised his glass in the air. All eyes turned to him. He stared at Sofie, unable to keep a grin from spilling onto his lips. Her big brown eyes narrowed on him while a scowl formed.

"We can't forget Sofie, now can we? To Sofie, for hanging around as a pretty face."

Alana and London laughed while Sofie slowly held her hand up and flipped him the bird. Jaxon chuckled and finished off the rest of his drink. This trip was much anticipated. It wasn't often that either he or London took time off from work. A vacation was just what they needed.

Having Sofie along was going to make it interesting.

# Chapter Three

Sofie wasn't going to think about Jaxon. She was going to enjoy her time in paradise. It was their second night on the island. She and Alana had spent half the day together treating themselves. They had appointments at the local spa. Sofie had indulged in a massage, manicure, and pedicure, and she even had one of those mud body wraps done. It was getting late, and Alana had retired to her bungalow.

London hadn't spared any expense. Sofie was certainly glad he had convinced her to let him pay for this trip. Her spacious bungalow was located over a lagoon. Every window gave her a breath-taking sight of the white sandy beaches off in the distance and the crystal-blue waters surrounding her quarters. She had never been anywhere as beautiful as this. This place screamed expensive, and she was sure the price tag would have taken a good chunk of her savings. Life as a registered nurse wasn't glamorous, nor did it allow her to afford such luxuries as this.

Hence why she was getting dressed to go out. There was a party for guests of the resort she wanted to attend. She hadn't come on this luxu-rious vacation to not enjoy the amenities. She was going to take full advantage of everything that came with their vacation package.

Sofie walked into her bathroom to assess herself in the mirror. It was still warm outside, so she chose to wear one of her new bikinis she had purchased for this trip. She chose a white suit that was sexy. The thin straps rested on her shoulders while the bottoms were high-waisted, showcasing her wide hips and ample bottom. She paired it with a bright-pink knit cover-up that fell to her mid-thigh.

"Okay, it's too warm to have my hair down," she murmured. She grabbed a hair tie and pulled her long, dark hair up into a ponytail. She left tendrils down at the base of her neck and around her face. After touching up her makeup and her lip gloss, she found herself to be perfect and ready for a night out. She smiled and hoped she could find a cute, single guy to spend the evening with. "You are such a whore."

She laughed and wandered through her bungalow and snatched up her small purse and rested the straps across her body to allow it to sit on her waist. She tossed her keycard into it, ensured she had money for tips, and was out the door.

A warm tropical breeze blew, caressing her skin. She walked down the few steps of her terrace to the wooden deck that expanded to all of the bungalows and led to the island. She took in the beautiful darkened sky littered with stars. The moon was high, and if she were a painter, she would certainly take advantage of this stunning sight and put it on canvas.

She arrived onto the white sandy beach that expanded for miles around. She sighed, loving this vacation. She already didn't want to go home. Eyeing the trail and the signage, she followed the instructions. The tall trees that she was sure provided shade during the day created a cozy feeling.

Sofie strolled along, admiring nature until she came to an opening. There were plenty of lamps highlighting the area, fire pits placed strategically around the wooden bars. The decor fed into the island 'getaway' vibe. A popular Bob Marley song played through the speakers as directed by the DJ whose booth was located off to the side. Sofie took in the crowd that seemed to be growing by the minute. There were tables and chairs strewn around, with waiters serving the patrons. This was an adult-only event which she was sure was appropriate. There were couples dancing on the makeshift dance floor that left little to the imagination as to what they would prefer to be doing.

Sofie smiled and made her way to the bar. She slid into one of the empty, round swivel chairs. The bartender was currently making a few drinks for a trio of women who were together. The girls seemed to be tipsy already. Sofie chuckled at their goofy antics and chatter.

The bartender, a muscular man who appeared to be a native of the islands, tossed her a smile. His dark hair flipped into his eyes. He jerked his head back to shift his hair out of the way. His arms were laden with tribal tattoo art. Sofie leaned against the bar and returned his smile. She was patient and could wait for him to finish serving his other customers.

Spinning around in her chair, she leaned back against the bar to take in the area. Her body swayed to the music. She sort of wished Alana was here with her. They had been best friends for years and always traveled together. But now her friend was married with a baby. She understood that Alana's priorities were her family. Sofie couldn't wait for that to be her. She just hoped it wouldn't take too much longer before she found Mr. Right. Then she and Alana could experience the next phase of their lives together.

But for now, she was single and would make the most of it.

The girls' gasps caught her attention. Their heads fell together as their chatter floated over to her.

"He is so fine," one whispered loudly.

"I'd definitely do him. No question about it," another said. "He looks like he's got a big dick."

"Bitch, please. He's coming back to my room tonight. Just ignore the screaming you'll hear," the third joked.

They fell into a fit of giggles. Sofie laughed at their conversation. They must be on a girls' trip.

Sofie's curiosity was piqued. She followed their gaze to the other side of the bar. She turned slightly and froze in place.

Jaxon.

Of course she couldn't get away from him. He sat smoking a huge cigar and held a small glass in front of him. He looked up and eyed the women who were not hiding their interest in him. There were two blondes and a brunette. They were dressed in skimpy outfits that revealed everything. Sofie was sure the blondes weren't natural, and from the looks of their bodies, they had all had work done. Were these the type of women who drew his attention?

"What if he wanted all three of us?" the first one whispered fiercely.

"What happens on vacation…"

"Stays on vacation."

Sofie shook her head. She wouldn't be surprised if he pulled all three of them. A sharp pain suddenly pierced her heart. She inhaled sharply, an unfamiliar sensation tingling through her.

Was that jealousy?

Sofie eyed the women again, this time seeing them in a different light. Her gaze went back to him. He tossed the women a smile, and she basically watched them melt in their seats.

Jaxon was shirtless, his muscles clearly defined. His dark hair was pushed back away from his face in a tousled style. It appeared as if he'd run his fingers through it. She bit her lip and held back a sigh.

It was obvious why the women were in a tizzy about him. He was drop-dead gorgeous and looked like a Greek god.

His gaze flickered and met hers. His lips curled up into a wide grin.

"Shit," she murmured. He'd caught her eyeing him.

He pushed back from his seat and lifted his glass. The girls' excitement grew. They were basically eye-fucking him as he walked around the bar.

"What can I get you, pretty lady?" the bartender asked. He stopped in front of Sofie, offering her a wide grin.

"I'll take a mai tai," she replied.

"Coming right up." He winked at her, glancing over her shoulder.

Sofie inhaled sharply and breathed in the scent of the smoky, sweet aroma of tobacco, leather, and wood. It smelled so good, she briefly closed her eyes before opening them. The women were now silently staring at her.

"Put it on my tab, Maleko," Jaxon said from behind her.

"Sure thing, Jaxon." Maleko jerked his head in a nod, turning away.

Jaxon took the vacant seat beside her. He finished off his drink and set the empty glass on the bar. He rested his body against the bar next to her. Sofie couldn't help the way her gaze drifted along his pectoral muscles that were scattered with light hair. She followed its trail down toward his shorts. She swallowed hard, recognizing he was all man. Hard muscles, little to no fat on his body.

"My eyes are up here, Sofie," he murmured.

Her gaze flew up to meet his, and she took in the cocky grin.

He lifted the cigar to his mouth and sucked a long drag, blowing out the smoke in the air. "If you're not careful, I'll start to think you're interested in what you see."

"I'm just trying to figure out where you got the audacity to invade my space and pay for my drink," she shot back. She was going to try her best to ignore her body's reaction to him, but that was proving to be hard. Her core clenched with need, and her nipples drew into tight little buds, rubbing against the soft cloth of her bathing suit.

"You're always busting my balls." He grinned. Raw heat and desire flared to life in his eyes.

Sofie was playing with fire. This she was sure of, but she was never one to back down from a challenge.

"Don't leave them out in the public and you should be safe." She shrugged.

Maleko returned with her drink and set it down in front of her. The peanut gallery had yet to tear their gaze from her and Jaxon. She toyed with the glass for a moment, lifting it to take a sip. It was made to perfection. Maleko was certainly heavy-handed with the rum, and she wasn't going to complain.

"My balls are fine where they are," he murmured. He leaned over closer, his lips brushing her ear.

She shivered, gripping her glass with both hands to have something to hold on to.

"But anytime you want to play with them," he said, "let me know."

"You'd like that, wouldn't you?" She arched a brow at him.

He lifted his head and grinned. He took another

hit from his cigar then set it down on the ashtray Maleko must have left for him.

After she took another sip of her drink, she jerked her head to the women who were still watching them. "I'm sure they would love to play with your balls and your little stick."

Sofie had to hand it to him. He hadn't taken his eyes off her since he'd arrived at her side. The smile slipped from his lips while his gray eyes narrowed on her. He moved closer, pressing his body to hers. A gasp escaped from her at the feeling of his warm skin against hers. She inhaled sharply, taking in the scent of his cigar and him. His hand slipped up to the back of her neck and held her in place.

Fuck.

A whimper came out, and she wasn't too happy about it. She didn't want him to know how much he was affecting her, but by the slight sound that rumbled from him—he knew. Jaxon lowered his head again, placing his lips near her ear. Whatever he was about to say, it was for her only.

"If I was interested in them, they would already be back in my place riding and sucking on my cock," he breathed. He tightened his grip and pressed his hips to her thigh.

Another whimper. The bulge she felt let her know that Jaxon Keith was anything but small.

"As little as you may think of me, I never play games, Sofie."

She swallowed hard, rendered speechless. Staring up into his eyes, she felt as if she were in a trance. Jaxon was weaving his web around her, and at the moment she didn't care.

"What do you have in mind?" she whispered.

His lips tilted up into a crooked grin. He released his hold on her and picked up his cigar. Now it was nearing the end, only a small part of it remained.

"What happens on vacation…" He paused, taking a drag from his cigar.

"Stays on vacation," she finished softly.

He had apparently heard the women speaking. Not that they were trying to keep quiet when they'd been making plans.

But it would seem she was the object of his desires tonight.

She had left her bungalow with the intent of having a good time and maybe even hooking up with someone. She even had the protection in her purse in case someone caught her eye.

She took another sip of her drink, thinking how

crazy it was that she was actually considering his offer.

Why the hell not.

Maybe what Alana had said was true. Maybe they needed to fight it out in the sheets.

Her mind was made up.

Jaxon would be the perfect person to expel her pent-up sexual need. It had been a while since she had been in the arms of a sexy man who had given her pleasure. Lately, her toys had been getting a lot of work.

Another sip, and she set her glass back down. She turned to him, her gaze sweeping his body again. She stood from her chair, her body sliding along his. She tilted her head back and offered what she hoped was a sexy grin.

"Just in case you didn't know, I like to dance." She moved away, ensuring her breasts brushed his chest. She held back a whimper this time and was proud of herself. She walked away, putting a little more emphasis into the sway of her hips. She felt the heat of his gaze on her.

The music was loud, and a good, slow-beat song flowed from the speakers. She threaded her way through the throng of people. Couples gyrated against each other to the rhythm. The lighting was low in the area. Her arms rose as she swayed and danced to the song. It didn't take long for strong arms to wrap around her waist and pull her back against a warm, solid body. She recognized the scent of Jaxon and his cigar.

She gasped, pressing her behind against the hardness of his cock. Moisture gathered at the apex of her thighs. He nuzzled the crook of her neck, his lips trailing along her skin. He moved with her, his body rocking with hers. His large hands splayed on her stomach, holding her in place.

"You're going to tease me, huh?" he whispered in her ear.

Even with the loud music floating through the air, she heard him. She turned her head slightly, meeting his heated gaze. She rocked her hips, thrusting her ass back into him. The slight intake of his breath was accompanied by a groan. His hand on her stomach tightened.

He nipped at her ear. "You are going to pay for that."

"Oh, will I?" She widened her eyes, trying to appear innocent, but Jaxon wasn't buying it.

"You most definitely will." His voice rumbled in his chest.

They continued their seductive dance. Sofie's

attention was on the man behind her only. The crowd of people faded. Everyone was lost in their own worlds. She leaned her head back to rest it on his chest. He was much taller than her, and his warm embrace had her body going haywire.

The music changed into another one that was sensual and seductive.

She bit her lip at the feeling of Jaxon's free hand slipping underneath her bathing suit cover. His warm palm skated over her thigh, drawing a moan from her. She reached up behind her, diving her fingers into his thick hair. His lips pressed against her neck, leaving a trail of kisses over her skin.

His finger ran along the fabric of her suit that covered her mons. She bit her lip, arching back against him. Her breaths increased as she tried to fight to bring air into her lungs. Her core clenched, screaming for release. Her senses were heightened, and the skin on her arms prickled from the goosebumps forming.

She pushed her hips forward, inviting him, almost daring him to make a move.

It wasn't long before he answered her unspoken challenge.

Jaxon's long finger slipped underneath the edge of her bathing suit and arrived at the hood of her pussy. She tightened her fingers in his hair. Jaxon boldly moved his finger to her slit. She spread her legs wider to grant him access and give permission. He took full advantage of her move and connected with her clit. Her pussy was drenched, and she wasn't ashamed of how wet she was. His finger was immediately covered with her arousal.

A groan tore from him. He scraped his teeth over her skin, sinking them into her. Not enough to break the skin, but just enough pressure was applied to send a jolt of electricity to her core.

His finger strummed her swollen bud. Her breath caught in her throat as he worked her over. She basked in the sensations coursing through her. His finger slipped away and dipped into her, coating him even more. He held her flush against him, his bulge rubbing against her. He slid his finger through her slit and returned to her swollen nub. She rode his hand, feeling wanton and desirable.

"Jaxon," she breathed. Her words were barely audible. Her climax was closing in on her. She inhaled sharply, her muscles growing taut. She was so close to orgasm. The thought that someone was watching them was like adding fuel to the fire of need burning deep within her. She bit her lip, desperate to feel Jaxon's large cock slide inside her.

"Mmm…I like the sound of my name on your lips," he murmured.

He nipped the lobe of her ear. His warm breath caressed her, sending her teetering on the edge. She arched her chest forward, her nipples hard and demanding his touch. The thought of his lips enclosing around her tight buds had her moaning softly.

"Your pussy's so wet, I'm betting you're wanting to come."

Unable to speak, she jerked her head in a nod.

His deep chuckle echoed in her ear. "Let me see what I can do about that."

He nipped her again then continued his sweet torture. She cried out softly, rotating her hips. He increased his pressure and sent her spiraling into bliss. She crested, riding the waves of her orgasm. Her head was thrown back while her moan was ripped from somewhere deep inside her.

Sofie leaned back against Jaxon, her muscles growing weak. A fine sheen of sweat covered her.

"Oh God," she whispered. Sofie couldn't think of one time she'd ever climaxed so hard. She opened her eyes and exhaled. Jaxon's finger continued gently stroking her. A shudder wended through her body. "Jaxon."

He withdrew his hand from underneath her cover. She immediately missed the feel of his large hand cupping her pussy. He spun her around and brought her flush to him. No one was paying them any attention. His cock pressed against her stomach. There wasn't much clothing between them, but for Sofie, it was too much. She wanted to feel his naked skin on hers.

With bated breath, she watched him raise his hand to his lips and slip his finger into his mouth. She groaned, resting her hands on his waist. Her breasts settled on him while she watched his eyes flutterer shut before opening. A rumble vibrated from his chest.

"Sweet as I knew you would be," he murmured.

He cupped her face and lowered his head to hers. He captured her mouth with his, and Sofie was a goner.

Whatever happened while on vacation was damn well staying on this vacation. She leaned into him and opened her lips. The kiss was demanding and passionate.

Jaxon lifted his head, releasing his hold on hers. He ran a finger along her bottom lip.

"Let's get out of here."

Jaxon led Sofie through the thick crowd. Once they burst free from all of the others, he tucked her into his side. He caught sight of the three women who had been goggling them at the bar. Their mouths dropped open as he guided Sofie past them. He didn't acknowledge them. He had the woman he wanted. Sofie had been on his mind, and from the moment he'd seen her sitting at the bar, he'd made a decision. He'd caught sight of a few other men who were near the bar eyeing her. The woman was beautiful, and he'd be damned if any other man was going to be tasting her tonight.

The taste of her still lingered on his tongue. He bit back a growl. He had thought he wanted her before, but now he was almost feral with the need to possess her.

He took notice of how well she fit into the crook of his arm. Her soft body was a direct contrast to his that was fit and solid. Sofie took care of herself. He knew from all of the times she'd tried to get Alana to go running with her.

She was still a woman who was blessed with curves in all of the right places. Her full breasts, wide hips, and rounded ass had his cock growing even harder. He grimaced from the pain of it pressing against his shorts. He eyed a path that would take them back to the bungalows that were positioned over the lagoon. There wouldn't be any time.

He needed her now.

"This way," he muttered. He directed them along the beach, eyeing the dark tree-lined area. The beach spread for miles, and the trees that joined it were thick and would give them enough privacy.

"Where are we going?" Sofie asked.

Her hand came to rest along the ridges of his

abdomen. He didn't think it was possible, but his cock grew even harder.

"Over there." He jerked his head toward a cluster of trees that were located along the beach. If she fussed, then he would drag her to his or her bungalow. She didn't offer any complaint, so he guided them over toward the trees. They broke away from the wooden path, his feet sinking into the thick white sand.

Sofie screeched, almost tumbling over at the same time.

"Where you think you're going?" He caught her hand and entwined their fingers together.

"Wherever you are taking me." She chuckled.

Her laugh sent a warmth rush of desire through him. It was husky and it always did something to him.

"But it looks like the sand wasn't having it," she said.

"Oh, nothing is keeping you from me," he practically growled.

He towed her behind him, leading the way. They weren't that far away from the resort nor the walkway that led to the bungalows. The high moon provided them low light. They passed the first tree, but he wanted them a little deeper but still close enough to the beach.

Jaxon pulled Sofie in front of him, backing her up against a stout tree. Her eyes were wide and locked on to him. He lowered his head, taking her lips in a deep kiss. He couldn't get enough of her taste. Her mouth opened, and he slipped his tongue inside. He rested his hand on the tree beside her head. He tilted his, deepening the kiss.

He had waited so long to get his hands on this woman, he wasn't going to waste time. He captured her moans while stroking her tongue with his. Her hands slid along his chest and down the ridges of his abdomen. He faithfully worked out to keep his body in top shape. The sighs and moans that slipped from Sofie as she traced every notch in his abdomen made him thankful he hadn't slacked.

He knew what he looked like. The amount of women fawning over him used to stroke his ego, but for some strange reason, the only woman he cared to know what she thought of him was Sofie.

Jaxon broke the kiss, breathing hard. His cock strained at his shorts, demanding to be released from his swim trunks. Sofie leaned back on the tree, not saying a word when he lifted her small purse and tossed it on the ground. Her pink cover dress was the next thing to join her purse. He closed the gap, resting his hands on her waist.

"Beautiful," he murmured, eyeing her.

Sofie's body was made for loving. Her small white bikini barely covered her mounds. He brushed her lips with his again. There was no time for much foreplay. That would be later. Giving her an orgasm while in the midst of a crowded dance floor was enough to have him teetering on the edge of his own release.

"Take me out of my shorts, Sofie."

She arched an eyebrow but didn't say a word. He moved his hands and placed them back on the tree. If he continued touching her supple skin, he couldn't promise to be a gentlemen. He'd throw her down on the sand and have his way with her.

He gripped the tree tight at the feeling of her soft hands sliding down his stomach. His abdomen trembled under her touch. She took her sweet precious time tracing the ridges of his muscles. He watched her hands come to his waistband. She pulled it away from his stomach and reached inside. Her small hands encircled his length.

"Oh my," she breathed.

She teased him, running her hand along his shaft once he was free from his shorts. The cool breeze blew, but it did nothing for him. His skin was warm with sweat forming on his brow.

"Jesus, how the hell are you walking with this thing like this?" she said.

"It's your fault." He sucked in air from the sweet torture of those small hands of hers running along him. They were smooth, void of any calluses. Her languid strokes were driving him close to insane. "I told you that you were going to pay."

"Really?" Her voice was low and husky.

From the look on her face, Sofie knew exactly what she was doing to him. Her fingers closed around the meaty head of his cock. She brushed away the drop of precum oozing from him. He bit back a curse and held off the thrust his hips wanted to make. Her hands slowly continued their perusal of him. If she carried on what she was doing, he'd been releasing in her hands, and that wasn't going to happen.

"Oh, yeah," he bit out through clenched teeth. He reached out with one hand and brushed her lip with his thumb. "On your knees, Sofie. I want those pretty lips wrapped around my cock."

Her eyes widened while her lips dropped open slightly. She didn't argue with him or put up a fuss. She wanted it just as much as he did. He growled watching her kneel in front of him. Sofie stroked him with her hand, guiding the tip of him to her lips. Jaxon spread his legs wide, holding on to the tree. He was afraid of what he'd do if he gripped her head.

Her mouth welcomed him, eliciting a groan to spill from his lips. Her mouth was warm and inviting. She pulled him in as far as she could take it, her hands wrapped around the rest of him. Her head bopped up and down, and she worked her magic with her hands.

Unable to resist, Jaxon cupped the back of her head with one hand and encouraged her to take him deeper. His hips thrust forward lightly. Jaxon didn't want to hurt Sofie, but her lips felt so good wrapped around his dick. The woman was a goddess, bringing him immense amounts of pleasure.

"Sofie, Sofie, Sofie," he murmured.

He tightened his hold on her head, his tilted back. The woman knew how to work him. Those small hands of hers slid along his shaft, her hot mouth continuing to take as much as she could. Her saliva coated every inch of him, the sounds of her soft moans reaching his ears.

Fuck.

She was enjoying this as much as he was. Her enthusiasm grew as the slurping sounds of her sucking him off increased. She had just started, and already he was on edge. A tremor snuck through him. He made the mistake of glancing down at Sofie and was hit with a hard burst of need. He was not going to last much longer. Sofie was about to snatch his soul from him.

Sofie's wide eyes greeted him. Her cheeks hollowed out, her head moving in tandem with her hands. At the moment she was the most beautiful woman he had ever had the pleasure of kneeling in front of him and sucking his cock.

A tingling sensation began in his balls and coursed through him. His breaths had turned into pants. Sofie's ponytail was destroyed by his grip. A shudder flickered through him. He was so close he thought it was only fair to warn her.

"I'm so fucking close, Sofie," he gasped. He pulled back on her hair to hold her in place to make sure she heard him. "You need to tell me now if you're swallowing or not."

The woman gave him a wink and went back to work.

He had his answer.

She was definitely a woman after his soul.

It didn't take much longer to reach completion. Sofie's hand took a hold of his balls, and he erupted. A roar escaped him as his climax slammed into him. The cascade of energy that barreled through him took his breath away. His warm release rushed from him. Sofie held his gaze with her mouth wide, accepting his creamy gift. Her hands continued to slide along his length, milking him for everything he had.

Jaxon locked his knees together to keep him in place. His legs had suddenly grown weak. He blinked a few times and could have sworn he had seen stars. He glanced back down at Sofie who had yet to release him from her hold.

"Come here," he growled. Jaxon helped her to her feet then pushed her back against the tree. He cupped her face and swooped down, capturing her lips in a brutal kiss. His semi-hard cock pressed against her stomach.

Sofie wrapped her arms around him and returned the kiss.

He needed more.

She was not leaving his presence until he'd had his fill of her.

Her soft lips drew him in. He tilted his head to the side to deepen the kiss. Her pillowy sighs had his dick growing hard again. Her hands skimmed over his chest and came to rest on the edge of his shorts. His dick twitched with him wanting to feel her touch again.

Jaxon bent down and lifted her by the back of her legs without breaking the kiss. Sofie settled her arms around his neck and her legs around his waist. She eased her face away from his. He buried his face into the crook of her neck. Her whimpers were soft and sexy. He braced her against the tree to allow him to reach between her legs and slide her bikini bottoms to the side. His fingers brushed her pussy, finding her drenched and ready for him.

"Jaxon," she whispered.

He parted her labia and nudged the broad head of his cock at her slick opening. Her wetness greeted him. Her thick cream coated him. He almost spilled from just the sensation of her pussy.

"This is going to be hard and fast," he gasped.

"Give it to me," she pleaded. She swooped down and sprinkled kisses on his face until she reached his lips. Their tongues dueled together in a long, seductive dance. She lifted her head, her lips ghosting over his. "I need you inside me, Jaxon. Now."

Any other day he would be pleased to have a

woman beg for his cock. But not Sofie. Her sweet plea would be rewarded after the way she had worshiped his cock with her mouth. He surged upward and swiftly entered her.

Their audible gasps filled the air.

If he had thought her mouth was paradise before, her pussy was heaven. He didn't hesitate, moving back and forth, guiding his cock into her warm, tight channel. Jaxon cupped her ass, holding her while he took full advantage of being inside her.

"Oh," Sofie groaned. Her head was thrown back with pleasure spreading on her face.

He lifted a hand and drew her top aside, revealing her two full mounds. Her warm brown skin was golden, highlighted by the rays of the moon. Her dark areolas captured his attention. His tongue wanted to glide along them, tasting her soft skin. He promised that later he would have his fill of them.

Jaxon had never known a desperation like what he felt now. His hips moved faster and faster as he fucked her. Sofie's grip on him tightened, her nails digging into his shoulders. He ignored the sharp little pain, focusing on nothing but the pleasure.

"Harder," Sofie gasped.

Her head fell forward, her eyes locked with

Jaxon. She rotated her hips, meeting his thrusts. He went impossibly deeper inside her.

Sofie cried out in ecstasy. "Just like that. Keep going."

Jaxon fucked her even harder. His movements quickened as he did what she begged of him. A low, guttural groan tore from him while Sofie's voice was hoarse with her louder cries. He couldn't care less that they were outside or that someone passing would hear them.

*Let them.*

He had a beautiful woman taking his cock, hard, just like he liked it.

"God, I'm about to come." Sofie's fingers slipped to the base of his neck. They dove into his hair and entwined with his thick hair. She held on to him, almost sobbing. "You feel so good in me."

There was a slight sliver of savagery that filled him. He wanted to watch her fall completely apart.

He gripped her ass and held her tight, brutally thrusting inside her. She threw her head back and screamed. Her pussy clamped down on him, sending a shudder through him. It pulsated around him, drawing out his orgasm.

He roared, reaching his climax. He strained, pushing deeper while he released inside her.

Jaxon's muscles grew taut, and there was nothing he could do but continue to pump his hips, filling her with everything he had.

Sofie's body grew relaxed. Her arms settled back down around his neck. She gently brushed soft kisses along his face until she reached his mouth. Jaxon's heart pounded, and he opened his mouth to her kiss. Sofie's tongue slipped inside. Normally one to dominate a kiss, he allowed her to control it.

Her body was soft and supple. Her breasts were crushed between them. His cock remained inside her, still semi-hard. He hadn't yet had his fill of her.

Jaxon had a healthy sexual appetite, but never had he had this type of reaction to a woman before. He wasn't ready to let Sofie go.

"Your place or mine?" he asked.

"Whichever is closest."

"Am I that boring to you?" Alana asked.

"What?" Sofie jerked her attention to her friend.

They were currently lying out on the beach, taking in the clear blue ocean. The girls were baby free as London and Jaxon had taken Chance with them.

Sofie yawned again and adjusted herself on the foldable lounge chair. Their two large umbrellas shielded them from the warm rays of the sun. Alana leaned forward and stared at Sofie suspiciously.

"You've yawned at least ten times in the last five minutes. What's up with you?"

"Nothing. I swear." Sofie waved her hand, dismissing her friend's nosiness. She laughed and prayed Alana couldn't see through her facade. She adjusted her sunglasses and pointed at the ocean. "That is the problem. Do you not hear the waves? This is my first vacation in eons, and I'm sorry that I'm yawning, but who wouldn't fall asleep where we are. I've worked double shifts for the past—"

"I'm sorry." A guilty expression crossed Alana's face. She leaned back in her chair and sighed. "You're right. I just want to make sure you are enjoying your time off. I didn't think that you would want to be a lazy beach bum on vacation."

Now it was Sofie who felt guilty. They were on day five of this amazing vacation, and she was having fun. Alana ensured they had participated in multiple excursions around the island, ate at the best restaurants, and experienced all of what Bora Bora had to offer.

Only Sofie wasn't being completely honest with her.

Every night when she 'turned in,' she had been with Jaxon. They had agreed to keep what was between them a secret. Every night she was fucked to within an inch of her life until the wee hours of the morning, meaning Sofie didn't get much sleep.

That man certainly had something to be arrogant and cocky about. It was no wonder the women chased after him. That long, thick cock of his was dangerous. Sofie could admit that she was becoming addicted to him.

The taste, the scent, and feel of him haunted her throughout the day. She couldn't wait for darkness to fall around the island. Once she separated from Alana, she became a little hussy, seeking Jaxon out.

Or he came to her.

For some reason or another, they couldn't keep their hands off each other.

"Don't worry about it." Sofie stretched her arms above her head and sighed. Even though the umbrellas shielded them from the sun, it was still bright out. A cool breeze came off the ocean, caressing her warm skin. It felt good with this tropical heat surrounding them. She finished her stretch and glanced at Alana who was staring at her.

"Come. Let's walk along the water." Alana stood from her chair and waited for Sofie to join her.

Sofie pushed off her chair and stood. She

tugged on her bikini bottom that had ridden up in the crack of her ass. She giggled and ensured the ties on her hips were still tight. Today, she wore a red suit that barely covered her breasts and showed off most of her bottom. She had purchased all of her swimsuits on a whim when they had started making plans for a tropical vacation.

When on a tropical vacation, why would one need to wear regular clothes? She had purchased enough to wear one for each day. Jaxon loved them.

Loved removing them, that was.

"Someone is trying to catch the eye of a man with that suit." Alana giggled.

"Whatever." Sofie rolled her eyes and joined her friend.

She hated to keep secrets from her, but she didn't think she could handle Alana's snarky remarks. If only her friend knew that she had finally given in and slept with Jaxon. Alana would never let her live it down. They walked down to the edge of the water. The warm, clear-blue ocean was welcoming. She was amazed at how clear it was. She could see the sand underneath it easily.

They began their trek, talking about some of their adventures they'd had on the trip. Sofie would love to come back, but she wouldn't be able to afford to unless she saved for a full year.

"Snorkeling was fun. We could do that again if you like," Alana suggested.

It had been an amazing experience. Neither of the girls had done anything like it before. The crystal-blue waters had held a whole other world that Sofie had been in awe of. The bright, beautiful colors had looked as if God had come down here and painted it himself. The many different fish, the living coral was an experience she would never forget.

"We could. But don't you want to do something with London without the baby? I could keep him for you so the two of you could enjoy the nightlife."

Alana released a snort. Sofie was feeling guilty again, thinking she could have been a better godmother to Chance. Alana rarely got a break. She was so stubborn and hated to ask for help.

"Well, to be honest, the resort offers a nanny service, and London was very persuasive in talking me into using it."

"That's awesome. Good for London. You deserve some time away from the baby and to spend it with your husband." Sofie relaxed slightly.

The waves crashed into her ankles. It was warm and inviting. She moved over to walk into it.

"When we were out, I stopped by your bungalow to see if you wanted to come with us." Alana glanced at her with a raised eyebrow. She wore cute blue prescription sunglasses that matched her navy-blue tankini.

Sofie swallowed hard, trying to keep her expression neutral.

"You did?" It must have been a night she was at Jaxon's. This would be the opening she needed to come clean to her friend.

Alana pushed her glasses up on to her head and squinted at her.

"So where were you? Is Stella trying to get her groove on with a young island man?" Alana questioned. She drew closer to Sofie and playfully nudged her with her elbow.

Sofie rolled her eyes at the movie reference.

"You never know, these men down here love some brown sugar," Sofie teased. She stumbled away slightly then ran ahead a few feet. If she misled her friend, then maybe Alana would leave her alone. She turned and walked backward, facing Alana.

"London said Jaxon has been whoring around down here." Alana snickered.

"Are we surprised?" Sofie needed to receive an Oscar for her performance. She hated lying to her friend, but it was for the best.

Alana caught up to her, kicking water in her direction. Sofie dodged out the way and returned the move. Alana squealed, jumping out of the way. Their frolicking led to more laughter and both of them being soaked. It didn't matter. With the current temperature, they would be dry again in no time.

"Why don't you invite your friend to come to dinner with us?" Alana asked.

The girls returned to their stroll. Sofie stiffened for a moment, her mind racing.

There was no way she could show up with Jaxon.

Nope.

"I don't think that would be a good idea. We're just having fun. I wouldn't want him to read anything in to it." It was amazing how the lie rolled off her tongue. Sofie breathed a sigh. She was going to have to atone for all of these lies. She absolutely hated doing it, but she had no choice.

"Oh, so it's like that? I didn't know you rolled like that," Alana teased.

"Hey, we're on vacation in one of the most beautiful places in the world. What happens on vacation, stays on vacation." She shrugged, trying to keep it light. A string of one-night stands was not her usual. She'd probably had one or two in her entire life. Sofie was a woman who knew what she wanted, and most of the men she'd dated recently didn't fit the bill. Her standards were high, and they just had a hard time reaching it.

She'd had boyfriends, but most of the relationships only reached a year. If she were to be honest with herself, what she had with Jaxon was exciting. She didn't know if it was the 'forbidden' aspect of things or how they were sneaking around, but she was thoroughly enjoying herself.

"Well, just be safe." Alana entwined her arm with Sofie's. She grinned and pulled her sunglasses back down over her eyes. The girl was blind as a bat and needed them. "We wouldn't want you leaving here with a stalker or an itch that requires a penicillin shot."

Sofie fell into a fit of laughter at her friend's joke. This was why she loved her so much. There was never any judgement between the two of them.

"I'll be fine. He and I have an agreement." Sofie fell quiet and turned her attention to the ocean. It was so peaceful and serene here. She never wanted to leave. Obviously, reality would be rearing its ugly head soon, and she'd have to return to her steady, boring life.

"Do me a favor. Snap a picture of him. I want to see what he looks like."

"For what? You have your own hunky husband, or did you forget you captured Mr. Hotness?" Sofie teased. It had been the nickname they had given London when he had first moved into the apartment across the hall from Alana.

"London has not let me live that nickname of his down since you told him about it." Alana chuckled. She pulled away slightly and ventured farther into the water where it rose to her knees. "You never answered my question. Snorkeling again?"

"Yeah, but this time, let's do the tour where we can snorkel among sharks and stingrays," Sofie suggested.

"Someone likes to live dangerously." Alana snorted. "But I'm down for it."

The girls had spent most of the day on a snorkeling adventure. Sofie was officially exhausted. She had enjoyed their time in the water. Swimming among sharks, stingrays, and other aquatic animals had been exhilarating. All Sofie wanted to do was take a hot shower and maybe lock herself away with Jaxon. That would have been a perfect way to end her day.

But that wouldn't be happening

At least not yet.

Alana had arranged for dinner for the four of them. So instead of making excuses, she'd agreed to go, then she'd gone back to her bungalow, showered, washed and styled her hair.

Sofie adjusted her dress. Every outfit she'd packed for this vacation was something she probably wouldn't wear in real life. She had been spontaneous when choosing this hot little number. It was backless and flowed around her thighs. A good wind would probably lift it and show everything God had blessed her with.

Sofie didn't have the heart to tell her friend no. Sitting down at a dinner table across from Jaxon would be hard. The things that man had done to her should be illegal. She'd never had a lover who was so demanding but yet attentive to all of her needs.

And the orgasms?

Life-threatening, world-shattering, leaving her craving another one.

The past week, Sofie had tried to appear as normal as she could be. But it was just so hard. How could she look the man in the eye and act like she hadn't ridden his face the night before? She was going to have to get herself together. Sofie was afraid Alana would sense something was different between them.

"It will be okay. It's just dinner," Sofie muttered. She applied her perfume and touched up her lip gloss. She looked like a million bucks. She turned around and glanced at her reflection, eying herself. Sofie was lucky in the ass department. She had a nice curvy one that was accented by the soft material of her dress. "Okay, girl."

She giggled and headed back to her bedroom. She chose a pair of strappy heels to wear along with a matching purse, then she was out the door. Dinner was sure to fly by, then she would go back to her place and await Jaxon's arrival. Tonight, Jaxon would be peeling her out of this dress. She could already see it. She grew breathless just thinking about his large, callused hands sliding over her soft skin.

Alana had chosen one of the popular restaurants they hadn't had an opportunity to try yet. It was located on the shoreline and even had options for dining on the ocean on a large yacht. Sofie had agreed to meet them there. With the cool breeze lazily tickling her skin, she breathed in the tropical air. This short walk would give her plenty of time to calm her excited body down. The minute she thought of Jaxon, her libido would go into overdrive.

Sofie tried to think of something that would take her mind off of how sexy the man was without any clothes on, or how talented he was with his tongue. Just in these last few days the walls she had constructed because of him were slowly falling away.

If she didn't know any better, she would think that she was starting to like him.

Maybe Alana had been right. They just needed to burn up all their frustrations between the sheets.

"Get it together, Sofie," she muttered. She arrived at the restaurant, appreciating its wood and textured thatched roof which went along with the island vibe, with the crystal-blue lagoon surrounding it. She'd heard wonderful things about this place and she hoped it lived up to the hype. She found Alana and London waiting at the bar. She hurried over to them, a smile spreading her lips. "Hey, guys."

"Yay, you made it." Alana returned her smile.

They shared a hug. Alana ushered her over to a free spot at the bar. London gave her a jerk of his chin, turning his attention to his cellphone.

"Where's baby Chance?" Sofie asked. Both of their arms were empty, and she didn't see any sign of her godchild.

"We hired a nanny for the night," London said, putting his phone away. He wrapped an arm around Alana's shoulders and pulled her close. He dropped a small kiss to the side of her head.

The two of them were so cute together, and Sofie could admit she was slightly jealous of the two of them. There was always a soft look between them, brief touches that didn't go unnoticed. London worshipped the ground Alana walked on.

What Sofie wouldn't do to have someone like that in her life.

"Only for a few hours," Alana said, nudging her husband. She turned her attention back to Sofie.

Slight disappointment filled her eyes. "So you weren't fibbing."

"About what?" Sofie frowned.

"Not inviting your um…newfound vacation friend." Alana slow-blinked her magnified eyes behind her stark-white frames.

"I said I wasn't." Sofie became slightly flustered, glancing at London.

He chuckled and turned away, flagging down a bartender. Sofie's cheeks warmed at the notion that he knew she was having a vacation fling with someone. She flicked her gaze to him before glaring at Alana who just casually shrugged.

"I'm sorry. I told him you'd found a friend here." Alana sheepishly picked at an invisible piece of lint on her long maxi dress.

"Why didn't you invite him? Embarrassed of us?" London tossed out over his shoulder.

The woman working the bar arrived and took their order. Sofie asked for a glass of wine. Tonight would not be a night she would want to have heavy liquor. There would be no telling what would come out of her mouth if she was drinking-drinking.

"Of course not," Sofie sputtered. She would never be ashamed of her friends. She and Alana had been friends for so long. They knew everything there was to know about each other—the good and the bad. It was just a complicated situation.

"Where is you know who?" Sofie leaned against the bar and tried to appear irritated. She had taken notice that London's twin was nowhere to be found. She casually peered around the restaurant, trying not to appear so suspicious.

The restaurant was suspended over water with an incredible view of the mountain off in the distance. It was very classy, and immediately, Sofie knew she was going to be in for a fine culinary experience. There were such rave reviews about the French and Polynesian dishes. The aromas in the air had her mouth watering.

"Oh, he's coming. We'll be seated once the entire party is here," Alana replied.

The bartender returned with their drinks.

Alana passed Sofie's glass to her. She jerked her chin to behind Sofie's shoulder. "Behave tonight, please."

Goosebumps appeared on Sofie's skin. It tingled, and she sensed an invisible caress along the curve of her spine. Her body only responded this way when he was around her. Jaxon was near. She raised her glass to her lips to hide the small smile that threatened. She turned and froze in place.

Jaxon was dressed in a tropical-themed, short-sleeved button-down shirt, and tan shorts revealing the sprinkle of hair lining his calves. His dark hair was brushed back away from his face as if he had combed it with his fingers. But it wasn't Jaxon's cocky grin that held her attention.

It was the long-legged blonde woman holding on to his arm.

Jaxon felt the daggers from Sofie's eyes and refused to look at her. He placed his hand on the small of Bindy's back and guided her over to London and the girls.

"You finally made it." London finished his drink and set the empty glass down on the bar behind him. "I thought I was going to have to send a search party for you."

"Yeah, I got your text. For some reason my phone didn't have reception," Jaxon replied.

London pulled him in for a hard hug with a loud slap on the back.

"You haven't changed," London murmured near his ear.

His brother stepped back and tossed him a wink.

London offered a hand to Bindy. "Hello there. My name is London. I'm the older, more good-looking twin."

"It's nice to meet you." Bindi giggled, taking his hand.

Her laughter was like nails on a chalkboard. Jaxon held back a wince. He moved back to Bindy's side and motioned to Alana.

"You may be older, but you are certainly not good-looking," Jaxon teased.

They were identical genetically. There were small things that made them stand apart. His parents were always able to tell the difference between the two of them. Everyone else, they reigned terror on. There were many times they had switched places and no one had known.

Bindy moved back to his side.

Jaxon motioned to the girls. "This is London's wife, Alana, and her friend, Sofie."

"It's so nice to meet you." Alana smiled, taking Bindy's hand for a quick shake. "I'm glad you can join us."

"It's a pleasure," Bindy replied.

Bindy turned toward Sofie, but she brushed past them with an unladylike snort. Sofie hit him with her icy-cold stare, and if it were possible, he would be pushing up daisies. Sofie was beyond pissed.

"Welcome," Sofie tossed out over her shoulder.

Jaxon bit back a smile and instead glared at her back. For someone who didn't want anyone to know about the two of them, she was definitely taking him bringing a guest to dinner wrong.

"I'm sorry about my friend," Alana rushed out. She motioned for Bindy to come with her. "Why don't we get you a drink before we're seated."

Bindy went with Alana while London eyed him.

"What?" Jaxon asked.

"What have you done to Sofie now?" London asked. His brother took a hefty sip of his drink and narrowed his gaze on him.

"Why is it that I am the one doing something to her?" he asked, feigning innocence. He moved to go to the bar. He was going to need a stiff drink to get through dinner.

London grabbed his arm and leaned in. "Look, I don't know what has gotten into the two of you, but y'all both have been acting weird since we got here." His face was void of emotions.

Jaxon knew the look. It was the older brother threatening look. He wasn't a child anymore and wasn't going to be intimidated.

"I don't know what you are talking about. I thought you wanted me to get along with Sofie?" he asked. London had been busting his balls for a while about the way he and Sofie were always at each other's throats. The few times they had all done excursions together, he and Sofie had behaved.

Now he'd done as his brother wished and London wanted to interrogate him about it?

London stared at him for a moment longer before releasing him.

"Get your drink. I'll let the host know we're ready for our table."

It didn't take long for them to be seated. Jaxon was between Sofie and Bindy. Sofie had yet to utter a word to him. Which it wouldn't have been too out of the ordinary before they came to Bora Bora. Now, he didn't know if he liked it.

He knew Sofie's body like he back of his hand. He had spent the last week sinking inside her, tasting her, and listening to her scream his name.

Now her silence was deafening.

The scent of her perfume reached him. He

breathed it in and felt a certain stirring beneath his waist. He had to keep his mind clear of any memories of him taking Sofie. It wouldn't do well for him to have a raging erection while at the dinner table.

Jaxon now regretted informing his brother that he was meeting women on the island. London had been insistent that he brought one of them to dinner. Jaxon didn't know London was going soft after getting married to Alana. All of the women they had fucked, it was rare for them to keep seeing them. The old London wouldn't have asked such a thing, but when London said that Alana was asking Sofie to bring her man, Jaxon didn't want to arrive alone.

Now that he saw that *she* had come alone, he felt like a royal ass.

He should have reached out to her earlier, but when he thought she was bringing someone, jealousy had reared its ugly head.

Jaxon Keith was never jealous. A man like him could have any woman he wanted. His eyes were drawn to Sofie. She plain ignored him. She stabbed her fork into her food harder than was necessary before bringing it to her lips.

His cock jerked again, and he turned away from her. He caught London staring at him with a raised eyebrow. Jaxon ignored the look and focused on his plate.

"So how did you and Jaxon meet?" Alana asked, breaking the short, uncomfortable silence.

"Simple story," Bindy replied. She wiped her mouth with her napkin and placed it back on her lap. She rested a hand on Jaxon's forearm and giggled.

Jaxon held back another wince.

"I go to the resort gym every morning and noted this handsome guy lifting weights," Bindy said. "I lift, too, and we struck up a conversation. The last few days, Jax has made my workouts fun."

"I'm so sure he has," Sofie muttered. She lifted her wine glass and took a hefty sip.

"What did you say?" Bindy looked around Jaxon so she could see Sofie.

Jaxon didn't miss the glare Alana sent Sofie.

"I said that's so nice of him." Sofie cleared her throat.

Bindy's face softened. "He's been the perfect gentleman," she exclaimed.

London, Alana, and Sofie all pretended to choke on their food and drinks. They fell into a fit of laughter while Bindy looked at them, amused.

"Really?" Jaxon snorted. He shook his head and bit back a grin.

They thought they knew him well. He could be a gentlemen when he wanted. Bindy had been correct. They had met at the resort's gym. He had seen a blonde with mile-long legs working on her squats while holding a twenty-pound dumbbell. He had gone over near her to grab a couple of dumbbells when he'd noticed she was crying while working out.

*"Are you okay?" Jaxon asked.*

*"I will be, I guess," the blonde replied. She sniffed and placed the dumbbell back in the rack with its mates. She scrubbed at her cheeks with her hands and stared at herself in the mirror. "I probably look horrible."*

*"You look fine for someone who obviously is going through something," he stated.*

*She didn't look bad, but there were red splotches on her face. Jaxon didn't do well with crying women or kids. He glanced around, but there were two other people in the gym, and they appeared to be together.*

*"Is there someone I can go call for you?"*

*She snorted and shook her head. She took her hair down from the bun and began fixing it. "To be honest, I'm supposed to be here with my husband for our honeymoon, but he ran off the night before we were to be married with his best man."*

*She turned to him with her red-rimmed eyes. "Am I stupid for coming here on my own?"*

*Jaxon immediately felt sorry for her. He could be an ass at times, but there was a good guy inside him. She was obviously hurting. One thing Jaxon respected was the sanctity of marriage. He had grown up with a wonderful example of a perfect marriage. His parents were still in love with each other after all of these years. He wanted that with his future wife.*

*"No, I don't think it's stupid for you to take a paid vacation that I'm sure you helped pay for. Why waste it?"*

*"He paid for everything." She sniffed.*

*"Even better," he joked.*

*That won him a smile.*

*"Hi, I'm Bindy." She stuck her hand out to him. When she smiled, she could be considered pretty.*

*"Jaxon," he said and took her hand in a firm shake. "Question for you. How did you not see what was between your ex and his friend?"*

*That earned him another smile. After that, they met at the gym and lifted together.*

"I'm not that bad," Jaxon muttered. Bindy needed an ear, so he'd lent her his. He would have to admit if he would have met her before coming to the tropics, he would have invited her out for a night of pleasure to keep her mind off her pain. But now all he could think about was the woman who sat next to him and had yet to speak with him.

So Jaxon did something the hadn't done before.

Befriended a woman he hadn't slept with

———

"Thanks for having me," Bindy said. She waved at everyone.

They were in front of the restaurant. London and Alana appeared to like Bindy. Sofie was just so damn stubborn. She had yet to speak to him. Each look he'd received held a threat to his life.

"Don't be a stranger while still on the island," London said.

"Goodnight," Alana said. She gave a little wave before turning to Sofie.

The girls entwined their arms and began walking away. London tossed him a wink then jogged after the girls.

"Come. I'll walk you to your bungalow." Jaxon rested a hand on the small of Bindy's back.

They left in the opposite direction. Bindy didn't stay too far from the restaurant. He would ensure she made it home safely, then he would head over to Sofie's to smooth things out.

He actually was looking forward to her anger and what was sure to be a fight. It was something about her fiery nature that made him want her.

"Thank you for inviting me out with your friends." Bindy strolled alongside him.

The moon was high, giving them plenty of light. It was beautiful out, and he found himself wishing it was Sofie he was walking with.

"Not a problem. You needed it."

"Was that her? The one who was angry?" Bindy slyly glanced at him.

He had shared with her that he was seeing someone but he was unable to tell anyone.

"Sofie?" He chuckled, sliding his hands in his pockets. He wasn't surprised Bindy had picked upon Sofie's animosity. At the gym the other day, he'd found himself telling Bindy about Sofie. It had felt good to speak someone. He was unable to confide in London. Since his brother had tied the knot with Alana, he was insisting it was time for Jaxon to do the same. Jaxon blew out a deep breath. Was he ready to settle down? "Yeah, it was her."

"Are you sure you're okay?" Alana asked.

She and London had walked her home. She glanced at them and shrugged.

"Of course." She laughed. Sofie ran her hands along the skirt of her dress, smoothing out the wrinkles. Taking a deep breath, she glanced up to meet Alana's curious gaze. She tried to erase all emotions from her face. She didn't want to be interrogated by her friend about this. "Why wouldn't I be?"

"You seem to be upset about something. Was it Jaxon and his friend?" Alana asked cautiously.

London strolled a short distance away from them as if sensing they needed a little privacy.

Sofie didn't want to admit how much it hurt her to see Jaxon with another woman. Had he been seeing other women during their time apart? They hadn't made any commitment to each other. Their only agreement was what happened here, stayed here. Sofie didn't know when she'd started catching feelings for him. This was supposed to be fun with no strings attached, but why did she harbor the distinct feeling of betrayal?

"I promise, I'm fine. I must have had too much wine. You know I can't stand his smug face and how he's flaunting his bimbos," she scoffed. She fiddled with her purse to keep her hands busy. As much as she wanted to strangle Jaxon, he was nowhere to be seen. He was with Bindy. She dug her hands into her purse in a strong grip. She didn't even want to think of what they could possibly be doing. "At least I didn't bring my guy, and what kind of name is Bindy?"

"Yeah, I don't know about her name." Alana chuckled. She glanced over at her husband then focused on Sofie. "But if you're okay, I'll head back to my place."

"I'm good, you guys enjoy the rest of your

evening." Sofie wrapped Alana up in a quick hug. She offered her friend what she hoped was a genuine smile before jogging up to her little bungalow. She entered and shut the door behind her. She leaned back on the wooden door and sighed deeply.

Sofie closed her eyes and couldn't shake the image of Jaxon and Bindy from her mind. Obviously, one woman wasn't enough for Jaxon. Sofie knew the type of man Jaxon was. He wasn't the settling sort of guy. He loved women, and she had made it too easy for him by caving in to the allure of his sex appeal and the electric tension that burned between them.

She had grown weak and had given in.

Well, no more.

She wouldn't be one of many while on their vacation. If he wanted Bindy and any other woman on the island, then he could have them.

Sofie opened her eyes and pushed off the door. She was a grown woman and would be fine. She knew what she'd signed up for when she'd started messing around with Jaxon.

"He's not the only person on this damn island who can have fun," she muttered. She tossed her purse onto the dresser and kicked her shoes off. There were plenty of options on and off the island for her. They'd had their fun, and it was over. Time to move on.

No more late-night visits or burning up the sheets into the wee hours of the morning.

She might as well end it now. It would be best she started detoxing and getting Jaxon Keith out of her system.

"I am not going home with hurt feelings. This was a vacation fling," she said. Hearing the words made her feel slightly better. She snagged her jammies from the dresser and paused. She could have sworn she heard a noise.

Was that someone knocking on her door?

"Oh, hell no. If he thinks he's coming here after being with that bimbo, then he has another think coming." Sofie tossed her clothes on the bed and stormed toward the front door. There would be no one else but Jaxon coming to her accommodation this late.

Sofie grabbed the handle and threw the door open. A growl rippled from her chest as she stared at Jaxon. He had the nerve to lean against the door-jamb with a cocky smile on his lips.

"Hey," he said.

"You have a nerve," she snapped.

He chuckled and pushed his way inside, past her.

She took a step back, watching him close the door. "Um, excuse me. I didn't say you could come in."

"You want everyone out there to hear us?" He arched an eyebrow at her.

He took a step toward her; she took one back away from him.

"I know you're upset," he said.

"Me? For what?" She held up a hand and shook her head. "Stay back."

"Seriously? You got on this 'fuck me' dress and thought I wouldn't have taken the hint?" He kept going until her hand pressed against his hardened muscles.

She swallowed hard, knowing what was underneath his clothing.

Her body immediately responded to his closeness. Her core clenched, and moisture collected at the apex of her thighs.

Dammit.

Her body was a traitor.

She backed away even more, but Jaxon continued on with a wicked gleam in his eyes.

"No one was sending you any hints. I might

have been trying to attract the eye of someone else," she taunted. Her back hit the wall near the doorway that led to her bedroom. Going in there would be a bad idea. Sofie knew what would happen if they ended up in there. She glanced to her left and could see the bed. She turned her attention back to Jaxon.

His gray eyes were locked on her lips.

"Is that so? You trying to tell me that someone else has been touching this body?" One of his hands came to rest on her waist. He crowded her with his body.

The scent of his cologne flooded her senses. She inhaled sharply, recognizing the smell of him. She didn't know the name of the cologne but had come to recognize it as Jaxon.

"Why would you care?" She lifted her chin and met his gaze.

Her body trembled slightly as his hand skated along her form and came to pause at her shoulder. He played with the tiny dress strap.

His gray eyes darkened, and his lips curved up into that crooked grin of his. His finger drifted onto her smooth skin, sending chills down her spine.

"Shouldn't I? You've taken my cock every night," he murmured.

Jaxon moved closer, dropping his head. His lips brushed her cheek when he leaned closer to her ear. There was no longer any room between them. His lips closed around the lower lobe of her ear in a short, hot nibble before he released it. His warm breath caressed her, and her eyes fluttered close.

"It's been my cock in your mouth and your pussy each and every night. You trying to tell me that I haven't been enough for you? You need more?"

"What?" Sofie swallowed hard again. It was difficult to concentrate with him overtaking her senses. Her legs grew weak. If it wasn't for him holding on to her, she would have slithered down to the floor.

"Do I need to repeat how you've taken my cock?" He pushed the strap of her dress down her arm. Then reached over and repeated the motion with the other side. The front of her dress fell down to reveal her bare breasts. His swift intake of breath was the only sound in the room. The cool air kissed her nipples, and they formed into tight little buds.

"No, you don't need to say it again." A shiver flew through her. She rested both hands on his chest and tried to shove him away from her. She had to put some distance between them. He had just left that blonde bimbo, Bindy. She blinked a few times, her anger swirling around in her. "What type of woman do you think I am? You were just with that blonde chick and then going to think you are going to come over here and put that dirty dick of yours in me after you've fucked her?"

"Bindy is not a bimbo." He chuckled.

He gathered her wrists in his hands and pressed them onto the wall. She struggled to free herself, but that just made it worse for herself. The damn dress slid down her body and ended in a pile on the floor, leaving her in nothing but a thong.

"Son of bitch," she muttered, staring down at her feet.

Sofie lifted her chin and eyed him. Jaxon did a slow perusal of her body, and the heat that flooded her felt as if he'd touched every part of her with his hands. How could she react from just a look? His grip tightened on her wrists.

"You honestly think that I would go fuck someone else, then come straight to you afterwards? Do you really think that I'm that guy?" he murmured.

There was something in his stare that made Sofie regret even mentioning it.

"You have a reputation, Jaxon," she stated. She

didn't back down from what she'd said. There was no denying it. He and his brother had been womanizers. She and Alana had watched all of the women who had come and gone from London's apartment.

He stared at her, not saying a word. She fidgeted in place, trying to free herself from his hold, but it did nothing but rub her nipples against his shirt. A moan slipped from her. They were so damn sensitive that it felt good to press them on him.

"You think you know me, don't you," he said.

He leaned down, nuzzling his face in the crook of her neck. He inhaled, breathing in her scent. She whimpered, turning her head away to give him more access to her. His tongue snuck out and slithered over her skin. He stopped right at her ear, nipping it with his teeth.

Tremors racked her body.

"You don't know a damn thing about me, Sofie."

Sofie turned her face toward Jaxon's. He captured her mouth with his in a hard, bruising kiss. She melted into him, returning the kiss with a heated passion. The tension between the two of them was palpable.

Jaxon commanded her. His tongue boldly

stroked hers, drawing it into a sensual dance. She moaned, unable to control her reaction to him. Jaxon knew how he affected her. It was no secret. From the moment he'd first kissed her, her body had no longer listened to her. It was as if it knew who it belonged to.

But it couldn't be.

When they returned to the real world, they would go back to their normal lives. Sofie squeezed her eyes shut.

He was right. She really didn't know him. Just knew what she'd seen before this trip and how well he knew how to work her body.

"I didn't fuck her. I haven't fucked her or anyone else since we've been here," Jaxon swore.

He leaned his forehead against hers. Both of them were panting, their rapid breaths the only sound in the room. He opened his eyes and met hers.

"You have been the only one I've been thinking about, the only one I want to fill with my cock." His voice ended on a growl. He released her wrists and rested his hands on the wall. His dark eyes studied her.

"Jaxon," she said. She placed her hand on his chest while the other slid along his jawline.

He leaned into her palm, heated desire burning deep into those silvery pools. "Tell me you believe me, Sofie. I may be many things, but I don't lie," he whispered.

There was nothing but honesty in his eyes. She had been so overwhelmed by her jealousy that she hadn't thought clearly. They had both alluded that they were seeing someone while on their vacation, and of course Alana and London would want to meet them.

Every ounce of anger and animosity had long ago drained from her body. There was one thing she had learned since meeting him: he was a good man with a big heart. She'd seen him in action with his nephew, and any man who loved kids was special in her book.

"I know," she replied softly.

Unable to resist, she slid her hand down his chest, unbuttoning the shirt as she went. Once it was opened, she tugged it down off his shoulders where it could join her dress. She paused on the waistband of his shorts. She slowly took in his perfectly sculpted form. She licked her lips, knowing what his skin tasted like. She'd spent multiple times running her tongue along every ridge of his chest, abdomen, and cock.

Speaking of his cock, Sofie's eyes were drawn to the hard bulge pressing forward against his shorts.

"What are you waiting for, Sofie?" Jaxon whispered.

His hands remained on the wall, but the way he'd enunciated her name, he might as well have caressed her skin with his hands. A rush of goosebumps appeared on her skin. Her fingers played with the button before opening it. She pulled down the zipper and slid her hands underneath the edge of his shorts, then pushed them down.

An unrecognizable sound escaped her when his cock sprang free. It was hard and standing at attention. His shorts fell, joining the other clothes. He kicked off his shoes and pressed her to the wall.

His lips captured hers in another deep kiss. Sofie wrapped her arms around his neck, holding him in place. His dick rested against her stomach between them. She ached to have it fill her. She loved how wide it stretched her out when he thrust deep inside her.

Jaxon reached down, lifting her by the back of her knees. Her legs automatically wrapped around his waist. He walked the short distance through the doorway over to her bed. He gently laid her down on the middle of it. He tore his lips from her and trailed hot kisses along her cheek and jawline. He continued on down her body, stopping at her breasts. She moaned, arching her back in the air. His hand molded around her breasts and guided her nipple into his mouth.

"Jaxon," she moaned.

Sofie dove her fingers into his thick hair. She loved how soft it was. He nipped her tight bud then soothed it with his tongue before giving attention to her other one. Sofie's legs were still wrapped around him. Her hips thrust forward, rubbing her pussy against his abdomen. She writhed on the bed, loving how he worshiped her body. While he licked and teased one breast, his large hand massaged and played with her other one.

He released her and continued his journey. Sofie's body was his playground. Each kiss sent a shudder of desire to her core. She was so wet, she could feel the traces of her desire on her thighs. Jaxon pushed her legs open, settling on the bed at eye level with her center. His heated gaze met hers, then he lowered his head. His fingers parted her folds, exposing her swollen clit. She arched off the bed, a cry ripping from her at the first touch of this tongue. He guided it through her entire slit, arriving at her swollen bud.

"Look at how wet you are," he breathed.

His finger rested on her labia, dipping into her wet heat. He pushed it inside her, her muscles closing in around him. He withdrew it and licked the digit clean. She groaned, watching his pleased expression.

"And you think that I need any other pussy when I have this one?"

Another stroke of his tongue. Sofie gripped the blanket beneath her. She widened her legs, wanting Jaxon to have full access to her. He peppered small kisses along her inner thighs, then returned to her pussy. He captured her clit with his mouth, suckling it.

"Jaxon!" she cried out.

Her hips lifted to meet him. He released her, his finger rubbing her swollen bundle of nerves.

"Tell me, Sofie. This pussy belongs to me?"

"No," she moaned.

"No?" He arched an eyebrow at her. His lips, moistened by her wetness, curved into a smirk. He pressed two fingers into to her opening this time.

A deep groan escaped her at the invasion.

"I want you to think of your answer again, Sofie."

"We agreed," she gasped.

His fingers sank deep inside her. She slowly gyrated her hips against his hand, taking her pleasure.

"We agreed only while we were here," she said.

"Do you still want that?"

His fingers set a slow, steady pace. She grunted, her head thrown back against the bed while her hips sought more than what he offered. Her core was needy and wanted more than his fingers. She wanted to feel the pulse of his thick cock pressing far into her.

Jaxon's lips closed around her clit again, and he continued to fuck her with his fingers.

Sofie cried out, unable to think. He was asking her an important question, but she couldn't form a complete sentence.

"Sofie, I asked you a question," he demanded.

"This isn't fair," she gasped.

"You will answer me," he growled.

"Not now," she pleaded. Talking wasn't what she wanted now.

"What do you want now, Sofie? If you don't want to have a conversation now, tell me what you want," he said.

The bastard. He knew what she wanted.

"I need to come. Jaxon, please. Make me come," she pleaded.

Sofie raised her head and met his gaze. His eyes were so dark, she could have sworn they were black. He lowered his head and feasted on her. Her cries and pleas filled the air.

Jaxon worked her body over, leaving her trembling, her words incomprehensible and weakening. He soon brought her to her climax, her body detonating. She screamed, her muscles tightening, her legs wrapping around his head while she flew to the heavens.

Sofie flopped back onto the bed a sweaty mess. Her eyes fluttered closed, and she attempted to regain control of her breathing.

But Jaxon wasn't done with her.

"Open your eyes, Sofie," he ordered.

The bed shifted as he crawled up her body. She did as he'd commanded and found him braced over her. He lifted her leg to rest it on his arm. Her orgasm had zapped the energy from her.

He probed her opening with the blunt tip of his cock. "I want you to see who is fucking you."

He pushed forward slowly, filling her. She inhaled sharply, the sting of her muscles stretching to accommodate his wide girth. Once he was completely submerged inside her, he leaned down, capturing her lips with his.

"Oh," Sofie gasped.

She reached up and rested a hand on his jaw. She was unable to tear her gaze from him as he withdrew slightly from her body before sinking into her again. He repeated the motion with a slight force.

"Yes," she said.

Jaxon's movements grew more frantic. She canted her hips, meeting his with each thrust. He repositioned himself on his knees, his hands resting on the backs of her thighs. This allowed him to go even deeper. Sofie cried out with each thrust, her body welcoming the hard fucking. Jaxon was taking what he wanted while also giving her so much more.

Another orgasm rushed toward her. With each thrust of his cock, it slipped over her clit. She could no longer hold back and felt herself fall over the edge of her next orgasm. Her body trembled and shook hard as the sensations of her release spread through her.

Jaxon wasn't long behind her. His roar filled the air, the warmth of his seed filling her. He fell forward, his massive warmth covering her. She wrapped her arms around him, holding him in place. She held on tight, never wanting to move from this spot.

Jaxon rolled them to where he was on his side and she was tucked into the crook of his arm. His cock had slipped from her, and she already missed the feeling of them being connected. He pressed his lips to her forehead and sighed.

"You're not changing your mind, are you?" he asked.

She already knew what he was asking. Sofie lifted her head and offered him a sad smile.

"What you said was right. We don't know each other at all. This is all we have," she whispered. She reached up and rested a finger to his bottom lip. She eyed them and bit back a sigh. Leaving what they had here on this island would be hard, but they would never be able to be more than what they had now.

"Then we make the most of it."

Jaxon stared at the spreadsheet on his computer screen and didn't see anything. It all blurred together. He blinked and shook his head. He'd been at work too long. He glanced over at the floor-to-ceiling windows of his LA office and took in the dark sky.

"Shit, where did time go?" he muttered. He ran a hand along his face and pushed back from his desk. He strolled over to the window and gazed out at the scenery below. Downtown Los Angeles was a mixture of soaring skyscrapers and rich culture. There was nothing like it. He watched the hustle and bustle below. Even though the sun had gone down, it was still busy.

Here it was, a Friday night, and he wasn't out on the town. It'd been six weeks since he'd left Bora Bora a changed man. The Jaxon Keith of the past would be out partying, wining and dining some pretty woman with long legs and plenty of cosmetic work. He had thought that was the type of woman he desired, but he'd discovered that wasn't the case.

He liked his women au naturel with big brown eyes, wide hips, thick lips, and perfectly melanated.

Jaxon ran a hand across his face. Since leaving the tropics, he had only seen Sofie in passing a few times. She had been avoiding him. It pained him to think that she hadn't wanted him. He never would have thought it would be him, pining after a woman. He'd had his share of women and never revisited any of them. It had been years since he had even attempted a relationship.

To think, the one woman he had contemplated starting a relationship with hadn't wanted anything more than the few stolen nights they'd had in secret. He had tried going back to his old ways, but each woman he'd taken out lacked something. He couldn't help it.

Jaxon found himself comparing all of them to Sofie.

He could have stayed in Cleveland, but he knew if he had, it would have been expected of him to be around his brother and family. With Sofie and Alana being best friends, she would have been there, too. So he'd decided to hop on their private jet and head out west to their California-based office. There had been plenty of work. Primetime Sports Management was growing at record speeds.

The shrill ringing of his cellphone bit through the air. He spun on his heel, tearing his gaze from the beautiful city life and snatched his phone up.

"Yeah," he answered.

"I hope I'm not interrupting anything," his older brother's voice greeted him.

Jaxon chuckled. If only London could see him now.

"You may want to sit down for this one," Jaxon said. He perched on the edge of his desk. Between the two of them, it had always been London who was the workaholic. Jaxon had learned so much about this business from him. Hard work led to being able to play hard, which Jaxon had always excelled in. "I'm still at the office."

"Holy shit. Who am I speaking with?" London joked.

Jaxon joined his brother in laughter. This was an uncommon occurrence that he found himself repeating as of late. He just couldn't keep his mind off Sofie, and to keep him occupied, he worked late and even on the weekends.

"Did you fall and hit your head or something?" London asked.

"Nope, not at all. There's just a lot going on here," Jaxon replied. He undid his tie and tossed it onto his desk. It was after hours, and there were no more meetings he was needed at. He opened the first couple of buttons on his shirt and folded up his shirtsleeves.

"And you know we have an exceptional team out in LA that can handle the work. You don't have to do it all on your own," London said, his voice becoming serious.

"Now it's my turn. Who are you and what have you done with my twin?" Jaxon snickered.

It would seem the tables had turned. He was the one who always berated his twin for working late and on the weekends. Marriage had turned out good for his twin. He now took more time away from the job and spent it with his family.

Jaxon yearned for what London now had. Only that would mean finding someone who was worthy of giving his last name.

Sofie's face appeared in his mind.

She was a good woman, strong, intelligent, and extremely sexy. Those nights spent between her thighs had become addictive. Their last night together, after having made love for a few hours, he'd just held her the rest of the night until the sun had risen. One last kiss, and he'd snuck out of her bungalow and made his way back to his.

"I had a wise man educate me that work will always be around," London said.

"So what's up? I doubt you are calling me just to see what I'm doing." Jaxon was curious as to the nature of this call. Not that he minded. They were as close as twins could be and spoke at least once a day. Jaxon took one look around his office and agreed with London.

Work will always be around.

He moved around, gathering his laptop and a few other things. He packed them away in his leather computer bag and left his office. The hall-ways of Primetime LA were empty. The sounds of a vacuum echoed through the air, alerting him that the cleaning crew was present.

"You never answered my invitation."

Jaxon pressed the button to the elevator. London had texted him a week or two ago about the birthday party he was throwing for his wife. Jaxon had yet to confirm because he knew without a doubt Sofie would be there.

"Invite?"

"You know what I'm talking about," London snapped.

Jaxon could hear the frustration in London's voice.

"What is your problem?" London asked. "We come back from Bora Bora, and I have barely seen you. It's like you're hiding out in LA. Did we do something to offend you?"

Guilt filled Jaxon. The elevator door slid open silently. He stepped in and hit the button for the private garage. The doors closed, sealing him in the small car. It wasn't like them to go too long without seeing each other. Growing up, they'd always been together. As twins, they shared a bond that was unexplainable. Jaxon sensed the hurt and confusion through London's voice, but he had to put some room between him and Sofie.

"Of course not. I've just had a lot on my mind," he admitted. He hadn't shared with London that the woman he had been seeing in the tropics was his wife's best friend. He'd never really kept a secret from him before, and it was killing him. London was in a relationship and would be able to offer him advice on what to do about Sofie. Hell, what to do about getting her to give them a chance.

This was all new territory for him. Jaxon was used to women tripping over their feet to be with him. He'd never had to pursue a woman in such a manner before.

"It doesn't have anything to do with that blonde from the island, does it?"

"No," Jaxon automatically replied.

Bindy was a good woman who had her own issues to deal with. Jaxon was just happy he was able to lend an ear and make her smile. Their platonic relationship would always remain on the island. They had not shared contact information before leaving.

"It's just some other shit. Nothing for you to worry about, big brother."

"Well, come to Cleveland. We can chill and work through whatever shit is bothering you," London suggested. Being the elder of the two, London always had to be the one to make sure he fixed whatever problems Jaxon had in life. "I got a new import of cigars that I'm dying to open but will only do it when you get here."

London knew his weakness. There was nothing like a good cigar, a glass of fine whiskey, and watching a game or movie. Their father and grand-father had introduced the boys to fine cigars when they'd been younger. Jaxon could still remember the first time he and London had sat around a fire pit with the elder Keith men enjoying their first cigars. As Jaxon grew older and wealthier, he could afford the imported cigars of countries from around the world.

"When is the party?" Jaxon asked. He stepped out of the elevator and made his way to his expen-sive sports car. He slid into the vehicle, and the aroma of fine leather assaulted him. He tossed his bag onto the passenger seat and turned the car on. His call immediately switched over to the hands-free option.

"Tomorrow, and I expect you to be here with a gift for Alana," London said.

Jaxon snorted. "Like she would want anything from me," he joked. He had purchased his sister-in-law a gift that he knew she would love.

"You better be here."

"I'll be on the first flight tomorrow."

"I'll send the jet to pick you up."

Jaxon grinned. If his brother was going to send their private jet to him, then the elder Keith meant business.

"Yes, sir. I'll be there with a gift," Jaxon promised. He would deal with the Sofie situation. If London wanted him there for his sister-in-law's birthday party, then he would be there. They disconnected the call, and Jaxon had to admit, he felt slightly better after speaking with him.

Putting his car in gear, he navigated through the garage and out onto the street. A few of the agents had invited him out for drinks. He had at first turned them down, but now he believed he would take them up on the offer.

———

"**G**lad you could join us." Brad slapped him on the back.

Jaxon had arrived at the nightclub that he and some of the other agents frequented. They were regulars here and had hosted plenty of clients at the exclusive club.

Even though it wasn't late yet, the crowd was thick. The music was thumping, and the air was electric. Jaxon turned around with his drink in his hand and leaned back against the bar. There were plenty of beautiful women, and hopeless men trying to gain their attention. The dance floor was packed with people moving to the beat.

"I figured I couldn't let you fuckers have all the fun," Jaxon teased.

Brad elbowed him, barking a hefty laugh. "Let me guess. You have to set an example as one of the bosses." He snorted.

"You know it." Jaxon laughed. He knocked back the rest of his drink, the burn of the alcohol sliding down his throat. He turned around and signaled for another one from the bartender.

She jerked her head in a nod, grabbing a bottle and strolling over to him.

"That was quick. Someone must be trying to party hard tonight." Her dark hair was pulled back away from her pale face. Her ruby-red lips curved up into a devious smile. Her shirt was low-cut, showing off her ample bosom. She leaned over onto the counter, putting her cleavage on display.

"Work hard, then it allows one to play hard," he replied. He turned around and pushed his empty glass toward her.

"That's a good motto to live by." She poured

him a hefty amount before lifting the bottle. She sent him a wink and leaned farther onto the counter. "I get off in an hour. I can always come by and help you party."

"My friends and I should still be here by then." Jaxon grinned and tipped his glass toward her.

She glanced down at another patron trying to summon her attention. "I'll look for you." She spun and walked away.

Her skirt barely covered her ass, and her heels were high. He had to get Sofie out of his mind, and it wouldn't hurt to start with a willing barmaid.

Even as he thought it, a foul taste appeared in his mouth. He took a sip of his drink and welcomed the burn of the expensive whiskey.

"Come on, boss man. Let's go join the others." Brad motioned for him to follow.

They arrived at the VIP section where other members of their team were gathered. The waitress was dropping off drinks for them.

"Put all of their drinks on my tab," Jaxon announced.

Their appreciative cheers went up in the air.

Jaxon lost track of how many rounds they had drunk. The music was blaring through the speakers, women came and went from their area. The bartender, Aimee, had joined him as promised. She sat next to him, leaning against his arm.

The night was full of entertainment. A few dancers came over and stood on their tables, thrusting and gyrating their hips to the beat of the music.

A night out was what Jaxon had needed.

"Hey, boss. Smile for the camera," Brent shouted over the music.

He held up his smartphone and snapped a picture. Aimee leaned into him, resting her head on his shoulder. He leaned back on the booth and spread his arms out behind him. Someone had gifted him a cigar. He held it in his left hand while bringing it up to his lips. Ashton moved on, snapping pictures of everyone else. Jaxon was feeling the effects of the alcohol.

"I love the smell of those things," Aimee said. She leaned completely into him, resting her hand on his chest.

"Is that so?" he asked. He inhaled, turning his head away from her to blow out the smoke.

"Why don't we get out of here?" She bit her lip, her wide eyes locked on him.

Jaxon stiffened. He couldn't even believe he was hesitating. Here he was, having a good night out with the fellas from the office, beautiful women hanging around with them and one even offering to take him home.

This should have been a win-win situation, but he just wasn't feeling it.

"I'd love to, but I can't," he found himself saying.

Her smile died, and she sat back away from him.

"Really? Like, are you married or something?" she asked.

"More like a something," he admitted.

"Oh, well damn. We could have had some fun." She recovered and smiled again. She reached inside her bra and pulled out a small piece of paper. She put it in his hand and enclosed his fingers around it. "Well, if that something turns out to be nothing, call me."

She leaned in and pressed a small kiss to his cheek. She got up and waved, disappearing into the crowd. He slid the paper into his pocket and reached for the bottle of whiskey sitting next to him. He lifted it and took a swig, turning his attention to the women dancing before him.

Yeah, he was going to have to do something about this Sofie situation.

"Are you sure you don't want me to help with anything?" Sofie asked. She folded her arms in front of her and leaned back against the island in the Keiths' kitchen.

"I'm sure. Everything has been taken care of," London assured her. He sat a box of wine on the counter and grinned at her.

Here it was, the day of her best friend's birthday party, and she felt useless. Apparently, London had taken care of all the details.

Their house was buzzing with decorators, caterers, bartenders, and waiters. There was literally nothing for her to do to help.

"I'll take Chance home tonight—"

"Nope, my parents are here and have claimed their grandchild," London said.

"How is there nothing for me to do?" She groaned.

She and Alana had gone for breakfast earlier that day and had got their hair done. Once they had returned home, she had scooped up baby Chance so she could feed him.

The chef who would be in charge of the food breezed into the kitchen and struck up a conversation with London.

She moved over to the windows that overlooked the backyard. She sighed, taking in the beautiful landscape. A large white tent had been constructed in the middle of the area.

"How about when guests arrive, you can just help with making sure everything goes over smoothly." London's voice snagged her attention.

She turned around and had to hold back a sigh. It was hard to look at her friend's husband.

He looked just like *him*.

The last six weeks since she had returned from the tropics had been hard for her. She had gone from having a dick appointment every night to no action at home except for her battery-powered toys.

Jaxon had tried to imply that they should continue their relationship once they returned back home, but she'd killed that notion. He wasn't being serious. There was no way a man who had women sniffing around him all the time would be serious about settling down with just one woman.

She'd saved both of them the heartache. What they had was a hot, steamy fling in one of the most beautiful places in the world. Things would have been different once they returned back to the States.

But she couldn't get him out of her mind.

So she'd thrown herself into her work. She'd picked up more shifts each week. Not that her bank account was complaining with the extra money coming in. Her body, on the other hand, didn't appreciate all the hours of sleep she lost.

"That's fine. I can direct traffic and stuff when people start to arrive." She sighed and left the kitchen through the patio doors. It was a gorgeous day outside. The sky was clear blue and looked as if it were painted by God himself. Not a single cloud was in the sky.

Inhaling the fresh air, she decided to do a walk

around the property. With the way she had been working, she hadn't really had a chance to go for her runs. She had been doing so good the last year, running a few miles three to four days a week. Glancing down at herself, she realized she'd gained some pounds. Her little pudge that she had gotten rid of years ago appeared as if it was trying to return.

Nope, not happening.

She'd done so good to lose the weight she had, she couldn't afford to gain any of it back.

"Come Monday, it's on. I will get back to running," she vowed. She would find a way to break this hold that Jaxon had on her. She hadn't even seen much of him since they'd left Bora Bora. From what she'd heard, he'd been spending most of his time recently in LA. She was sure he had probably moved past her by now.

A man like him, good-looking and rich, didn't stay alone for long, and living in a city like Los Angeles gave him ample amount of women to choose from.

Sofie sighed again. Maybe she should start dating. There were plenty of decent men out there. She just had to find them. Some of the girls at work had been begging her to come out with them.

Maybe next time she'd take them up on their offer. She wasn't much of a party girl, but it would be hard for her to meet a man from the couch in her living room.

Well, that was, not using those dating websites. She'd heard of people having success using them. She pulled her phone out of her back jean shorts pocket and swiped the screen.

Could she seriously do online dating?

She opened up the app store and typed in a name for one of the popular dating sites. She downloaded the app.

"I must be really desperate," she muttered. The program opened, and it required that she set up an account. She found herself on the side of the house where a small stone terrace was located. Sofie perched herself on the stairs and stared down at the screen.

What could it possibly hurt? She could just create the account and skim it to see what was out there.

Following the instructions, she filled out the questions that appeared. When it came to the part where it asked for a photo of herself, she paused. Her hand shook slightly at the thought of someone out there being able to read her profile and gaze upon her picture. Would someone find her appealing? Would there be any interest in her?

"What the hell is my problem?" she muttered. "I am one hell of a catch."

She giggled and clicked on the blank photo space that opened up her photos on her phone. She scrolled them until she found one that she was happy with. Her breath caught in her throat when she realized it had been a selfie she had taken in Bora Bora. The crisp blue skies and ocean behind her were beautiful. The sun was shining down on her, giving her a natural glow.

She uploaded the photo and laughed again. She was going to have fun with this. Even if she didn't find anyone, she would have a blast browsing. Maybe even a couple of bad dates could be entertaining for her.

"What are you over here for? And laughing by yourself?"

Sofie jumped at the sound of Alana's voice. She glanced over to find her friend staring at her with her hands resting on her waist.

"I don't even know if I want to tell you." Sofie chuckled, holding her phone to her chest.

Her friend narrowed her eyes on her suspiciously. Alana would not understand the idea of online dating.

"Oh boy." Alana strolled over to her and took a seat by her on the steps. "I'm starting to feel some kind of way. You are keeping more secrets from me?"

"I am not. I explained to you about Bora Bora." She sighed.

Alana had questioned her unmercifully about the guy in Bora Bora, but Sofie had held strong and kept her mouth shut on the details. Sofie leaned into Alana and showed her the screen of her phone. Alana pushed her glasses up on the bridge of her nose and squinted.

"Is that…" She threw her head back and howled with laughter. She snatched Sofie's phone out of her hand and stood with tears streaming down her face. She turned around and faced Sofie. Her smile faded as she took in Sofie's expression. "Oh, you're serious."

Sofie didn't know what came over her. She had been giggling herself about filling out the form, but now that it was someone else laughing at her, she didn't find it so funny. She was actually hurt by the way Alana found the fact that she'd joined a dating website so hilarious.

"I am," she said softly. Sofie pushed her long thick hair behind her ear. She glanced down at her hands, unsure of herself. Maybe the dating website wasn't the best idea. "I think I'm ready to find someone. It's lonely out here, and I figured I'd try online dating."

"I'm sorry. I didn't mean to laugh at you. I thought you were being silly and I…" Alana flew to her side and sat back down next to her. She handed Sofie her phone. Her large eyes were magnified by her glasses. "Please don't be mad at me."

How could she stay mad at her friend? Alana wouldn't even harm a fly. She had been by Sofie's side through all her failed relationships. Sofie softened at Alana's expression.

"It's okay," Sofie said. She rested a hand on Alana's thigh. She gave it a squeeze then let her go. "I never thought I would be on one of those sites, but here I am."

"What happened with the guy you were hooking up with in Bora Bora?" Alana asked. She turned to Sofie with hope in her eyes. "I may not have gotten the chance to meet him, but you certainly had a glow to you that I haven't seen in a long time."

"Yeah, because I was getting my back blown out

nightly." Sofie snorted. She had to make a joke of the situation. "Me and him agreed to end everything when we left."

There was a certain pain in her heart that appeared which she tried to ignore. She had her doubts on whether or not she had made the right decision. Those nights she'd had with Jaxon would forever be burned in her memory.

"Tell me about him," Alana asked softly.

"Well, he was very handsome and so sexy. We met at one of the bars one night when I had decided to go out for a drink. All the women were eying him, but he kept staring at me." She embellished the story of the night Jaxon was at the bar smoking a cigar and the three women trying to get his attention.

Alana's eyes grew even wider while she listened to Sofie's story.

"You skank!" Alana gasped. She shoved Sofie with her elbow. "So you slept with him the first night y'all met?"

"It was so worth it," Sofie murmured, remembering their first time as if it were yesterday. She had never been one for public sexual display, but there was something about Jaxon that had her falling to her knees. "That man had me begging for him to touch me."

"And you're sure it's over between the two of you?" Alana asked.

"Yeah. It is." Sofie blew out a deep breath. She offered a smile and motioned to her phone. "But I'll be okay as soon as I find another Mr. Right. Maybe it's time for me to have a ho phase."

"Speaking of ho, my brother-in-law arrived while we were gone, and he's three sheets to the wind drunk." Alana shook her head.

"What?" She hadn't realized that Jaxon was in the house when she had walked through it. The place had been quiet aside from the workers trying to get the house ready for the party. London hadn't looked as if he was pissed off when she'd spoken with him.

"London laid into him for showing up still hungover from whatever party he was at last night." Alana swiped her finger on her screen. She shook her head and sighed. "I told London I didn't think they should put things like this on social media."

She held up her phone for Sofie to review it. Sofie took it from her. The pounding in her heart echoed in her ears. She bit her lip and stared at the pictures of Jaxon and guys from the office out at some club. She hadn't seen Jaxon in a few weeks and had even blocked him from hers so she wouldn't be tempted to stalk from afar.

But the photos she gazed upon revealed that he had indeed moved on from her. There was a beautiful woman attached to his side who barely had clothes on. His arm was around her, and they looked as if they were real cozy.

"Is that his girlfriend?" she asked. Her throat tightened as the question spilled from her lips. His crooked grin, mussed hair that looked as if someone had run their fingers through it, and familiar cigar in his hand, brought about a pain in her chest that she was unfamiliar with.

"Girlfriend? Probably some chick he hooked up with last night." Alana snickered. She took her phone back and closed the app. She pushed off the stairs and stood. "Come on. You can help me pick out which dress I'm going to wear. I have two that I couldn't decide on, and I need your expertise."

Sofie stood and followed her friend around the house. If she had her doubts on whether or not she had made a mistake in shutting things down with Jaxon, she'd got her answer.

London had gone all out for Alana's birthday party. Her friend deserved to have someone so devoted to her. Sofie hadn't seen her so happy. She couldn't wait for the day she found a man who loved her just as much as London loved Alana.

Sofie grabbed her champagne glass and stood from her table. The party was in full swing, and the dance floor was packed with people line dancing to a classic song.

"You're not going to go out there and cut a rug?" Larry Keith asked.

She had the pleasure of sitting at the table with the Keith brothers' parents and her family. Alana had practically been adopted by Sofie's family.

Sofie glanced back at the crowd and saw her parents in the middle of everyone having fun. Her brother, Joey, had disappeared a while ago with a few of Alana's cousins. Tonight's soiree was like a mini family reunion. The record changed to an upbeat country song, and people paired off, enjoying themselves.

"I don't know this song." She chuckled. She drained her glass and placed it on the table.

"This is a goody," Larry said. He pushed back from the table leaned over and dropped a kiss to his wife's forehead. "Be back, honey. I'm going to show Sofie here how we do it down South."

"You can't run from him, my dear. He loves to dance." Donna Keith laughed. She had Chance resting on her shoulder, patting him on his back. The couple was wonderful and kept everyone laughing with stories of London's and Jaxon's younger days. Apparently, the boys kept them busy. "Go have fun, my dear."

"I'm not the best dancer," Sofie lied.

Larry snorted and took Sofie by the hand and led her to the designated dance floor. The elder Keith certainly had moves. Sofie was impressed with him. Larry kept her laughing. He twirled her around, and Sofie barked a hefty laugh. She soon found herself clapping along with everyone as the DJ spun another upbeat party country song. Larry guided her by hand in turns and shuffling to go along with everyone else who seemed to know the dance that went with the song.

"See, there's nothing to it," Larry said.

There was a twinkle in his gray eyes that were so similar to his sons'. His charm rivaled the twins', and Sofie now knew where they got their swag and personality from.

"You're a good teacher." She giggled. She felt as

if someone were watching her. She glanced over at Donna who was standing, dancing in place with Chance. She scanned the area and didn't see anyone staring at them.

Sofie's gaze landed on the person standing behind Larry. Her smile slowly faded as she met his heated gray eyes.

Jaxon.

He had cleaned up. She had heard he had crashed in one of the guest rooms, sleeping off his stupor. His hair was combed back away from his freshly shaven face. He was dressed in a black button-down shirt and jeans. Sofie's heart rate skyrocketed with just a look from him.

"May I cut in?" Jaxon tapped his father on the shoulder. His dark smoldering eyes held Sofie's.

Larry spun around, holding Sofie's hand. "I see you decided to join us in the land of the living," he said. He placed Sofie's hand in Jaxon's. He offered Sofie a wink and a crooked grin. "A few dances was enough for me. I'm not as young as I once was."

"Thank you, Larry. It was fun." She sent him a wink of her own.

He gave her a nod and disappeared into the crowd.

Jaxon brought her flush to him, the song

streaming through the speakers now a slow one. The sun was beginning to go down, the sky littered with impatient stars showcasing their bright lights. Strings of small electric lights were lined underneath the tent ceiling, casting a soft glow around them.

"Don't be flirting with my father," Jaxon murmured. He pressed his lips to her temple.

Sofie tried not to melt against him. As much as she didn't want to admit it, Jaxon felt so good. His hardened muscles were a deep contrast to her soft frame. He was tall enough where he could rest his chin on top of her head if he so desired.

"He is a happily married man," he said.

"His wife gave her blessing," Sofie taunted softly. She tilted her head back, a small smile finding its way to her lips. She was supposed to be angry and upset with him, but one look and feel of him, and all of that vanished. "Your mother was occupied by a very handsome young man who had all of her attention."

They swayed to the music, falling into a strained silence. There were so many questions that sat on the edge of her tongue, but she didn't ask any of them. She dropped her gaze to the top button of Jaxon's shirt. His large hands rested on the small curve of her back while the other one held hers, lightly resting on his chest.

"How have you been?" Jaxon's voice rumbled deep in his chest.

Sofie inhaled sharply, breathing in his cologne. She fought the urge to nuzzle her nose into the crook of his neck and breathe in more of the scent. In Bora Bora, she had gotten so used to the smell of him. In the few moments since being back in his arms, she was immediately transported back to those nights being wrapped up in them.

She wouldn't admit out loud that she missed it and she missed Jaxon.

"I'm good. Working a lot of shifts at the hospital," she replied. She would keep it short and sweet. That was a safe answer. She was having a hard time concentrating with the feeling of his hard erection resting against her stomach. Her core clenched with need, but it was going to have to wait until she got home to pull out her handy-dandy battery-operated friend.

Her dry spell had started again. Six weeks since she had felt the touch of a man. Sofie decided she would begin her search through the app. If she played her cards right, it might take her a couple of weeks to find someone who may not be a serial killer, maybe four to six weeks' worth of dating before sex.

Great.

One to two months before she could possibly have sex again.

And to think it may not even be decent sex.

Sofie stumbled, tripping over Jaxon's feet at the realization that she might as well invest in a lot of batteries.

"Sorry about that," she gasped.

Jaxon's hands tightened on her. She glanced up and found his heated gaze on her. Sofie's breath caught in her throat. She had forgotten how captivating his gray eyes were. Her nipples grew into taut little buds. She bit back a groan and resisted the urge to rub herself against him.

"How about you?" Her voice sounded breathless. Sofie found herself trying to pull away slightly from Jaxon. The last thing she wanted to do was embarrass herself here with tons of friends and family surrounding them.

"Working a ton also," he murmured.

A frown formed on his face. He drew her back to him possessively. A small noise escaped her at the hold he held on her. There was no space between them. She whimpered, her arousal growing. Moisture collected at the apex of her thighs. She didn't even have to check to see if her panties were damp.

"Where are you going?" he asked.

The DJ transitioned to another slow song. Sofie glanced over at the DJ booth. She had hoped he would put on a fast song that would give her an excuse to escape the intimate hold that Jaxon had on her. Being this close to him had her body going haywire.

"It wouldn't be appropriate for us—"

Jaxon's snort interrupted what she had been about to say.

"What would be inappropriate would be sliding my hands underneath this dress of yours." His lips brushed her ear.

She squeezed her eyes shut, remembering the last time he had done that. Her breaths increased heavily, almost to a pant.

"We shouldn't, Jaxon," she breathed. She tried to pull away again, but he held her firmly to him.

"You say we shouldn't, but I know that you feel me and how much I want you." He nipped her earlobe and moved his hips forward, ensuring she felt the bulge in his pants.

"Do you want me? Or just what I have?" she asked. She tilted her head back to look him in the eye. The images of him on Alana's phone came racing back.

"What is that supposed to mean?" His grip on her hand tightened. He narrowed his gaze on her, studying her face.

"Look, Jaxon. I know what type of man you are. Yeah, you have needs, but that doesn't mean that it's just for me."

"Sofie, what the hell are you talking about?"

"Did you want that chick who was hanging on you at that bar? Did you fuck her?" She broke free of his hold and hated how she sounded. But she couldn't help it. If he truly wanted her, why had he stayed away from her? Why hadn't he pursued her?

"Sofie." He ran a hand over his face and took a step toward her. "Let's go somewhere and talk."

"No, Jaxon." She shook her head then spun on her heels, dashing through the crowd. She tried to breathe in but found she was having a hard time pulling in air.

She needed to leave.

Sofie ignored the sound of her name being called and kept going.

Jaxon released a curse, unsure of what he had done to upset Sofie. He stalked into the house, finding his mother standing in the kitchen with Chance who was sitting in his high chair.

"Hey, Jaxon." Her smile disappeared the moment she took one look at him. She spooned some food into Chance's mouth before setting the bowl and spoon on the island. "What's wrong, baby?"

He hadn't seen his mother when he'd first arrived at the house. At least he hadn't thought he had. Jaxon would admit, he'd drunk and partied way too hard last night. He barely remembered walking onto the jet that morning.

The moment he'd arrived at his brother's place, London had laid into him.

*"What the fuck? This is how you show up for my wife's birthday?" London hollered.*

*Jaxon winced, London's voice adding to the throb of his brain.*

*"What are you talking about?" Jaxon mumbled. The world appeared to turn on its axis, and he stumbled.*

*"And you smell like a fucking brewery." London snagged him by his arm and led him into the house.*

*"I had a little fun last night. We missed you. You should have come." Jaxon grinned at London who scowled at him. They went up to the second level of the massive home, with London practically carrying Jaxon up the stairs. "Top-notch drinks, women—"*

*London slammed Jaxon against the wall, holding him by the collar of his shirt. Jaxon's smile disappeared when he took in the seriousness of London's face.*

*"That's not who I am anymore," London growled.*

*"What are you talking about?" Jaxon leaned his head back against the wall. It had always been him and his brother. They did everything together. He quickly sobered up at the look in London's eyes.*

"I've grown up, Jaxon. I would suggest you do the same." London released him and took a step back from him.

Jaxon made an attempt to straighten his shirt, but it was a skewed and half-buttoned.

"I am grown," Jaxon mumbled.

"We are thirty-seven years old, and you act like you're twenty-one," London said. He motioned to Jaxon. "You need to do better. We are getting older."

"What? You want me to be like you?" Jaxon snorted. He pushed off the wall and moved to stand in front of him. They were identical in every way except a few scars that each had received due to sports in their youth and random tattoos they had both gotten over the years. "I'm not perfect like you. I don't have the big house, the beautiful wife and son."

"Perfect? My life is far from perfect." London reached out and grabbed him by the arm. He led him down the hallway into one of the guest bedrooms and shoved him in.

Jaxon stumbled and spun around to face him.

"Strip, shower, and get some sleep," London said. "You need to sober up for the party."

"You don't get to tell me what to do," Jaxon grumbled. He began unbuttoning the shirt the rest of the way and shucked it off onto the floor. He turned and headed toward the attached bathroom. It was the room he usually slept in when he stayed in town. London had sold the apartment he had kept downtown. For a while, Jaxon had used it when he was in Cleveland.

"I've always told you what to do." London smirked.

"Fuck you." Jaxon waved a hand at him. In his drunken stupor, he pushed his pants down, tripping over them. He crashed to the floor.

"You are so fucking drunk. If I wasn't pissed at you, I'd be laughing and recording this," London murmured. He came over to Jaxon and helped him from the floor. "Let's get you in the shower. Mom and Dad should be arriving any minute."

A piece of paper was on the floor in front of Jaxon. He picked it up and squinted at it. He snorted and handed it to London.

"I am being responsible at my age," he bragged. He waved the paper around in the air. "If I wasn't, I would have gone home with Aimee here."

"And why didn't you?" London asked, snatching the paper from him. He bent down and helped free Jaxon's feet from his shoes and pants. He stood and guided Jaxon into the bathroom and over to the shower stall.

"Because that's not who I want," Jaxon admitted. He clamped his mouth shut, having already said too much.

London's eyebrows rose high, his curiosity piqued. "And who might that be?"

"None of your damn business." Jaxon flipped the shower on, adjusting the temperature until it was perfect. If he let on *that it was Sofie who had been on his mind, London would never let him live it down. He turned to his brother and smirked. "You can go now, unless you want to be reminded that I have the bigger dick."*

*"In your dreams." London rolled his eyes and turned, walking out of the room. "If you vomit and mess up this room, I will kick your ass, then make you clean it up."*

Jaxon blinked, having missed part of what his mother said.

"I'm sorry, what did you say, Ma?" he asked.

"I said, what's got you looking all gloomy?" She stepped over to him and wrapped an arm around his waist.

He pulled her in for a tight hug and breathed in her scent. His mother had worn the same perfume since he was a little kid. It immediately comforted him, and his muscles relaxed slightly.

"Nothing I can't handle," he murmured.

She stepped back from him and eyed him wearily. "Sure. I've seen this face before when you were younger. It's about a woman, isn't it?" She raised an eyebrow at him.

Chance used that moment to cry out, slamming his fist on the tray in front of him. Jaxon chuckled at his nephew. Apparently, he was impatient and hungry. Jaxon could relate to the little man. He was the same way when he was starving.

"Looks like you are taking too long." Jaxon laughed.

Chance looked at him and offered him a grin, showcasing the two tiny teeth that were present on the bottom row.

"Oh, hold your horses," Donna said. She turned back to Chance and scooped up a bit of his food on his spoon and offered it to him. "Now go ahead and tell your mother what the problem is."

Jaxon wasn't going to get off on this one. His mother was still riding high on the fact that one of her boys was married and had given her a grand-baby. If Donna Keith had her way, he and London would have about five kids each. She had been on him ever since she'd met Alana. If London could find someone to put up with him, then he could, too.

"Okay, fine. There is a woman," he began.

"Aha! I knew it." Donna exclaimed. She grinned, her eyes twinkling as she danced in place. "Your brother said you mentioned something about a woman. Now tell me all the details."

Jaxon sighed, running a hand over his jawline. He didn't know when his twin had become a gossip.

It violated the twin code. As much shit as they'd got in to as kids, they had never ratted each other out.

"It's not much to tell. We haven't even been on a date yet or anything," he murmured. He paused and realized the issue. Sofie's comments set off a light bulb in his head. She thought he only wanted her for her body and the sex. Not that the sex was a bad thing, it was amazing between the two of them. He'd never experienced anything like that with any other woman in the past.

"Well, what have you done—" Donna paused and raised a hand. "Don't answer that. I already know the answer. Well, no wonder you're having issues. If it's a woman you are interested in, you probably put the cart before the horse."

"I'm seeing that now." He moved over to her and took her by the shoulders. He laid a kiss on her forehead. "Love you, Mom. I got to go."

"Love you, too, babe."

He ruffled the hair on Chance's head before dashing out of the kitchen. He had to find Sofie. He was sure she was somewhere on the property. She wouldn't have had much time to get in her car and leave.

Now, he just had to find her.

It didn't take Jaxon long to find Sofie. She was sitting on the swings of the playground that London had built for Chance. It was on the opposite side of the house to where the party was being held. It was positioned near a patch of woods that ran along the side of his brother's home.

He approached quietly, slowing down as he got near. Sofie sat in the swing, slowly rocking back and forth, looking down at her hand. From the light emanating from her hand, he assumed she was scrolling on her cellphone.

He paused and inhaled softly, trying to gather his thoughts. He wasn't sure how she knew about last night or what female she was speaking of. There was no way she would know about the chick from the bar. He vaguely remembered someone taking pictures. He cursed himself for getting so sloppy drunk. There was no excuse for it.

"Sofie," he said quietly.

She cried out, startled. Her phone went flying through the air. She stood and spun around to face him. They stared at each other for a moment. A gentle breeze blew by, sending her hair into her face. The only sound aside from the distant music floating through the air was the screech of metal from the swing moving back and forth on its own.

"Um, Jaxon," Sofie said.

He walked over to her and reached down, picking up her cellphone. He glanced down at the screen and frowned.

"What is this?" he asked.

She stiffened slightly. She snagged her bottom lip with her teeth and shrugged.

"What do you think it is?" She stood to her full height and squared her shoulders.

He glanced back down at the phone and saw a profile of a man. He moved the screen down, taking in the guy's stated interests, hobbies, and career.

"Is this a dating app?" he asked. His heart pounded at the thought of her searching through one of these online companies to find a man.

Someone who wasn't him.

Had she already found someone? Did she like what she saw in this guy's description? Something he was unfamiliar with reared its ugly green head in his chest.

Was this jealousy?

Fuck, yeah, it was.

Sofie was his.

He blinked. This was the first time he'd actually

claimed her. He thought about it for a moment and knew that he meant it. She had filled his thoughts for so long, and he loved getting her riled up. The culmination of their arguments since they'd met had been a form of foreplay. When they had come together, it had been explosive.

"Yeah, and?" Her chin rose defiantly.

Something in him snapped.

He strode toward her and grabbed her by the back of her neck. His head lowered, and he swooped down and took her lips in a brutal kiss. His tongue swept inside the moment she parted them. Sofie's muscles tightened under his hold for a brief moment before melting against him. Her hands slid up his chest and locked together at the base of his neck.

Jaxon eased back slightly. The sound of Sofie's whimper excited him. She wanted this as much as he did. He lifted a finger and tilted her chin up to force her to meet his gaze.

"Is this what you want?" he asked, bringing her phone up so they both could see the screen.

She rolled her eyes and tried to pull back from him, but he held on to her.

"Jaxon, it's none of your business," she murmured.

He ignored her, reading the potential candidate's profile out loud. "Chad Martin. Thirty-five years old from Akron, Ohio, who loves dining at fine restaurants, jogging along Lake Erie, and traveling around the world."

"Jaxon, stop reading," she pleaded and tried to take the phone from him.

He held it out of her reach, swiping to another potential candidate.

"That one not good enough for you? How about this one? This guy, Dr. Terrance Clayton, is an internal medicine doctor who loves hiking, skydiving, and traveling. Looking for a good woman who shares the same interests."

Sofie's fist landed on his stomach. He swung his gaze to her, stunned. Did she really just hit him? She broke loose and stepped back from him.

"What are you doing, Jaxon?" Her eyes narrowed on him. It was a familiar look she always had when she was pissed at him or was about to argue with him. She shoved him with her small hands before coming to stand in front of him.

"Are you done making fun of me?" she asked.

"Making fun of you? I'm helping you." He snorted and motioned to the phone. His annoyance flared thinking how she hadn't even considered him. The chemistry between them was off the charts, and the sex had been mind-blowing. Everything about her had him only thinking of her. "Obviously you have something better in mind."

"Better in mind? Better than who?" she snapped.

"Me," he growled. He reached out to her automatically, bringing her to him. He crushed his mouth to hers, unable to resist touching and kissing her.

She belonged to him.

She softened, returning the kiss with the same fever. Her fingers latched on the hair at the base of his neck. He growled, needing more of her. She broke the kiss, her breaths coming out in pants.

"Jaxon," she murmured.

He didn't want to give her a chance to think of anything else but him. He tilted her chin up, forcing her to look him in the eye.

"Me. Give me a chance," he said.

She licked her lips, drawing his attention to her swollen mouth.

He wanted to take them again, but he resisted. "Let's start over. Me and you."

"But what about the woman from the pictures?" She frowned, her body stiffening against him.

"What pictures are you talking about?"

She snatched her phone from his hand, muttering to herself. He kept his arms around her, not wanting to let her go. She felt perfect in his embrace. As much as he wanted her naked, writhing underneath him, he was going to have to be patient.

"These photos." She held her phone up for him to see the popular social media site.

He blew out a deep breath. It was from the previous night. He shook his head and lifted a finger to her face. He gently stroked her chin and ran a finger along her cheeks.

"Nothing happened with that woman. She was hanging out with us. I'll admit I was drunker than I should have been, but I didn't go home with her even though she asked."

"Why?"

"Because I was thinking of you, Sofie. I can't stop thinking of you," he admitted truthfully. He had to be honest that he hadn't even missed having sex with other women. It was getting old, and his brother was right. He needed to grow up, and if he wanted to settle with someone, he wanted it to be with a good woman. Someone strong, smart, funny, and adventurous.

That woman was currently in his arms.

"Are you serious?" she whispered.

He lowered his head toward hers. She reached up and cupped his jawline. He leaned into her palm, closing his eyes briefly.

"I've been thinking of you, too," she said.

"Then why the dating site?"

"Because I thought you had gone back to your usual self." She exhaled and leaned forward, resting her forehead on his chest.

He ran a hand along her back, savoring the feeling of her relaxing in his arms.

"I figured if he could move on, so could I."

"Is that why you wouldn't even let me mention us continuing to see each other? You thought I would be seeing other women along with you?" He snorted, then raised her chin again so he could meet her eyes. "Listen, the women I've messed around with weren't my girlfriend or anything. They knew what they were getting into. It was for fun. Nothing serious."

"I'm not looking for just fun, casual sex, Jaxon. I want more."

Her admission took his breath away. Was he seeking more? He knew without a doubt he was. Something in him had changed. One-night stands were no longer appealing to him. He wanted to wake up next to the same woman every day. He wanted to experience life alongside someone who made him smile, challenged him, kept him aroused.

"So do I." He lifted her hand from his face and brought it to his lips. He pressed a kiss to it and offered her a wide grin. "Let me take you out. A good ol'-fashioned date."

She blinked, staring at him before a smile lit up her beautiful face.

"You better be on time. I want to be wined and dined. And I don't want to be taken somewhere you've taken one of those—"

He swooped down and captured her lips again to quiet her. Sofie didn't know what was in store for her. When he wanted something, he put his mind to it. She'd better hold on tight.

Jaxon Keith was officially pursuing her.

"Are you sure you don't want me to take you home, baby?" her father asked.

"Don't worry, Dad. I have a ride home." Sofie gave her father a hug as they stood next to his car. Her mother was already in, sitting in the passenger seat.

"Well, all right. Don't forget we are going to grill out at the house next weekend." He pressed a kiss to her forehead.

"I should be able to make it." She laughed.

Her father loved cooking out, and his grilling was infamous. He slid into the car and gave her a wave. She spun around and walked a few rows over to an expensive sports car.

Jaxon leaned against it, waiting for her. Alana's party was beginning to wind down. She hadn't driven this morning when she and Alana had gone to breakfast and the beauty shop to get their hair done. London had gone all out for Alana and had them chauffeured in a luxury limousine. She at first was going to spend the night in one of the guest rooms, but she'd changed her mind when Jaxon had offered to take her home.

"And whose ride is this?" She hefted her purse on her shoulder, folding her arms in front of her. She eyed the vehicle and knew it would be too costly for her nurse salary. She kept forgetting the Keith brothers were loaded. Their business was definitely booming by the looks of his ride.

"Mine." Jaxon's cocky grin spread wide. He pushed off the car and moved to the passenger door and opened it for her.

She raised an eyebrow and ambled over to him.

"What?" he asked.

"Nothing." She slid into the supple leather seat and exhaled.

He shut the door and came around to the driver's side. He got in and shut the door. They were basked in darkness. The scent of real leather and new car assaulted her.

"So you keep cars here, but you don't live in Cleveland?"

He turned the engine on and maneuvered it through the row of cars parked on the lawn. With the amount of guests that had showed up for Alana's party, everyone had parked in the large yard in front of the mansion. Soon, Jaxon had guided the car onto the paved driveway and headed toward the road.

"Well, I was staying at London's old condo until he decided to sell it. I didn't have much here since his place was furnished. So when he sold it, I just moved my things to their house."

"And you hadn't considered moving here, or is LA your home?" she asked quietly. This question had popped into her head the second he'd shared with her that he was interested in more. The butter-flies in her stomach fluttered. Could she do a long-distance relationship? California and Ohio were not close at all, and the time difference could be brutal.

"I've considered it. Ohio is definitely much cheaper to live than LA. With the office there, London and I have always rotated between here and there. LA is exciting, but it can get old quick," he said.

"I've only been there once," she murmured. She turned in her seat slightly to face Jaxon. His dark hair fell forward toward his face. Her hand itched to push it away from his forehead.

"Maybe one day I'll take you," he replied. He glanced over at her.

Sofie's core clenched at the heated look he sent her.

"There's plenty to do there," he said.

"We'll see. I do have some extra vacation time put away." She grinned. She settled back and glanced out the window. She didn't want to get too excited about any future trips or plans.

One day at a time.

That's what they were going to do. They were going to start dating.

But if they were going to officially start dating and have their first date, did that include sex?

Sofie glanced back over at Jaxon and clenched her legs together. Her core pulsed with the thought of his thick cock. She held back a whimper, remembering how well they fit together.

"What are you thinking about?" he asked. He guided the car onto the highway. It was late, and there weren't many vehicles on the road. The car accelerated, the scenery flying by. Jaxon's crooked grin was noticeable in the low light.

"Nothing at all," she murmured. She took the time to study him while he drove. His hand rested on the gear shift while the other one guided the car along.

"Doesn't look like nothing," he replied. He glanced over at her before turning his attention back ahead of them.

"Why me?" she asked. He could be with any woman in the world but instead he was here with her. Since the moment they'd met, there had been something about him. She thought he was handsome, but his arrogance was downright annoying. They argued over everything, but now she saw that it was a way of foreplay.

"Why not you?" He snorted. "If I had the chance to submit what I wanted in a woman, you would be the end result. You are beautiful, intelligent, sexy, funny, and caring. The list could go on. Everything about you is just right for me."

Her heart thudded.

Jesus.

The man certainly knew which buttons to push for her. She bit her lip and realized it was the same for her. If she had the chance to input what she wanted in a man, Jaxon fit the bill.

"You're just saying that."

"Am I? If I didn't want to be with you, I wouldn't."

"Are you sure? I'm not like any of the women you were with before?" She scowled at the memory of the women she'd seen him with. The first time they had ever met, he'd been staying at London's old apartment and had been hosting a party. There had been no telling how many women had been there that night.

"That's a good thing." He reached for her hand and brought it to his lips. He pressed a gentle kiss to the back of it. "There is no other woman like you. Those other women can't hold a candle to you."

Sofie bit back a smile and tried to not fidget. She was completely turned on by his words alone. Mr. Arrogant was turning into Mr. Smooth Talker.

She turned away and stared out the window at the scenery as it flew by. They rode in a comfortable silence. They sped along the dark road until he took the exit that would lead to her home. It wasn't long before he was pulling into her driveway. She lived in a quiet, safe suburb on the east side of Cleveland.

He killed the engine and turned to her.

"Want to come in for a nightcap?" she asked. She didn't want the night to end. It was late, but she wasn't tired at all. Inviting him in was a setup. They were supposed to be having their first date soon, but asking him in for a drink was just payback for bringing her home.

A drink would be sufficient for a ride home.

Jaxon's intense gaze had her swimming in her seat. The corner of his lips lifted into a smirk.

"I was hoping you'd ask." He exited the car and came around to her side and opened the door for her. He held out his hand and assisted her out. He shut the door behind her and entwined their fingers together as they headed up the walkway toward her porch. Her home was a small brick house that had been fully renovated before she had purchased it.

They arrived at her door. She took her hand back from Jaxon's to allow her to dig inside her purse in search of her keys. Jaxon leaned his shoulder on her home, watching her. She giggled, finally finding her keys. She took them out and held them up.

"How much stuff do you have in there?" He snorted.

"All the things I need." She slid her key inside the lock and twisted. She glanced over at him and smiled shyly. She wasn't rich and loaded, but she was proud of her home. She had worked hard to be able to afford it. "Welcome to my home."

Sofie pushed the door in and entered. Jaxon strolled in, his eyes immediately scanning her place. She shut the door behind him and turned, trying to see things from his view. There was an open floor plan that allowed the kitchen to be in view of the living and dining room.

"I have some wine in the fridge." She brushed past him and tossed her purse down on the table beside her couch. Her automatic timers had switched on the living room lamp. She had purchased the system when she rotated shifts at work. She hated coming home to a dark house.

"Where's your bathroom?" Jaxon asked.

"Down the hall, first door on the left."

He jerked his head in a nod and strolled down the hall, disappearing from her sight. She flew into the kitchen and went over to the fridge. She opened the door and reached in for the bottle of wine she'd purchased, saving it for a special night.

Having Jaxon in her home was definitely an occasion that called for wine.

She set the bottle on the island in the center of the room, moving over to her cabinets to find two glasses for them. She stood on her tiptoes and pulled them down. She moved back to the bottle and remembered she'd purchased a cheap one. She loved her five-dollar wine from the local grocery store. There was no cork to fight with, just a good ol' twist cap.

Sofie opened the wine and poured two glasses. She took a hefty sip from hers and exhaled. Two warm arms surrounded her from behind. She leaned back into Jaxon's embrace. His strength radiated around her. She could stay here in the circle of his arms forever.

"What you got there?" he asked. Jaxon nuzzled her neck, his breath skating along her skin.

"Pinot Grigio." It was one of her favorites. She loved the light taste of the crisp, dry wine. It was chilled to perfection. She didn't like too-sweet ones, and this was always one of her go-to favorites.

"I've always been a red man myself, but I'd be willing to try it." He scooped her glass from her hand and lifted it to his lips.

"Hey, that's mine." She spun around in his arms, watching him down the rest of what was in her glass. She rolled her eyes at him. "You are not to gulp wine like you're taking a shot."

Jaxon shrugged and placed the empty glass down on the counter behind her.

"That's pretty good." He gathered her close to him. His head slowly lowered toward hers. "But I have a taste for something else."

Sofie's heart thundered. She leaned into Jaxon, already forgiving him for taking her drink. His warm lips molded against hers, his tongue probing her mouth. He tasted of her beloved wine, a hint of pear, apples, and plum. She kissed him back, returning the intensity and surrendering to his hold over her.

Sofie gripped his shirt tight, not wanting him to move away from her. A fire was lit inside her, starting at the tips of her toes and spreading through her body. She whimpered, his hard cock pressing against her. She strained into him, wanting to feel him naked.

Jaxon's hand came to cup her face, and he angled his head, deepening the kiss. He backed her up until her spine touched the island. He broke the kiss and trailed open-mouthed kisses along her jawline and neck.

Her fingers went to his shirt, and she unbuttoned the top few ones that she could reach.

"Jaxon," she murmured.

"Fuck, Sofie. I said we'd have our first date, but I can't keep my fucking hands off you," he growled. He lifted his head and stared down at her.

Sofie trembled at the look of feral passion in his eyes.

"I don't want you to keep your hands off me," she admitted. She finished opening his shirt and pushed it off his shoulders. Her hands immediately went to his undershirt and tugged it over his head, revealing his perfectly sculpted pectoral muscles. She sighed, running her fingers along the ridges of his abdomen. She followed the small trail of hair that was sprinkled on his lower stomach.

"Is that so?" His hands slid over her bare thighs and disappeared underneath her dress. He got rid of her panties, dropping them on the floor.

Her dress and bra was next, leaving her naked. The cool air met her skin, but she didn't feel it. Her body grew flushed from the look of approval in his eyes.

"You're so fucking perfect."

He gathered her to him, capturing her lips again. This kiss was different. It was full of need, desire, and heat. Sofie turned her pleasure over to Jaxon. Her body knew who was in charge. His hands slid over her body, caressing her, fueling the fire burning inside her.

Her thighs were slick with the evidence of her need for him. The caress of his fingers on her bare skin was maddening. She needed more of him.

"Jaxon," she whispered his name again.

He lifted her and placed her on the edge of the island. She leaned back, resting her hands on it while he put his attention on her breasts. She gasped from the slight pain of his teeth. She arched her back, offering herself to him. He suckled, licked, and nipped her mound, trailing his tongue along her chest to the other one. His large hand gripped the one he'd abandoned while his mouth covered her other nipple.

Pleasure raced through her. She hadn't realized how sensitive her nipples were until he gave them the attention they had been craving. Her pussy ached with need. It was already prepared for his invasion. Her core clenched in anticipation of his thick cock pushing deep inside her.

Sofie dove her fingers into his thick hair, holding him in place. The way he worshiped her breasts had her ready to melt into a puddle on her countertop.

Once he had his fill of her full mounds, he moved farther down her body.

"Lie back, Sofie," he commanded. He pushed the bottle and glasses out of the way.

She immediately lay back on the island, spreading her legs wide.

She didn't have to be told to do this.

She wanted it.

Needed to have him feast on her.

She closed her eyes, a shiver ripping through her. His large callused hands slid up her inner thighs. Her muscles quivered; he ran his fingers along the seam of her lower lips. He pressed a kiss on each of her inner thighs.

A moan slipped from her; his warm breath caressed her pussy. His finger slipped inside her slit, tracing the full length of her.

"Fuck, Sofie. You're so damn wet," he murmured.

His finger was soon replaced with his tongue. A gasp escaped her. Her hand shot out, her fingers burying themselves in his hair once again. She held on to him while he took his first taste of her.

He arrived at her clit, suckling it gently at first but soon increasing his pressure. Her cries pierced the air from the sensations surging through her. She tried to arch her hips up, but he pushed her back down.

Sofie moaned low at the feeling of his finger gliding inside her slick channel. He slowly fucked her with that digit while he continued his assault on her swollen nub. Sofie was drenched, his finger easily slipping inside at her moan. Her muscles clamped down on him.

Jaxon grunted, introducing a second one, stretching her channel open wider. Her body writhed on the kitchen countertop with the immense pleasure flowing through her.

Sofie's eyes flew open when a hand came down on one of her breasts. The man had a talent for multitasking. He teased her nipple, squeezing it and playing with it. The onslaught of stimulation sent her toward the edge of her release.

Her body shook, the need for her orgasm spiraling through her. His name spilled from her lips as she chanted it. She could take no more and dove straight over the cliff into ecstasy.

Her muscles tightened, her legs clamping on his head. She reached her orgasm. Stars aligned in her sights. She screamed, her body no longer under her control.

She flopped back down on the counter, panting

and unable to move her limbs. Jaxon lifted his head from in between her thighs. She opened her eyes and took in his glint in his eyes and knew he was not done with her yet.

---

Jaxon's hands went to his belt. He opened it and then removed his pants. His cock was straining to be released from its prison. The scent and taste of Sofie would be forever burned in his brain.

He eyed her, lying before him with her legs still splayed wide. He took in her warm brown skin, her full breasts, and her glistening pussy still dripping from her release. He pushed his pants and underwear down, kicking his shoes off.

Pride filled his chest. He knew that she'd had a hard orgasm. From the way her muscles had tensed, the tightness of her grip on his hair, the sounds flowing from her as she'd crested.

Jaxon licked his lips, once against tasting her release on his tongue. He couldn't take his eyes off her center. Her slick pussy was his haven. Jaxon gripped his thick erection in his hand, stroking it. He looked at her opening drenched in her sweet honey. He took a hold of her ankle and tugged. His cock was heavy and ached to be within her slick walls.

She slid from the counter, and he took a hold of her body and guided her down to where she stood before him. Her big brown eyes watched him. He couldn't resist capturing her lips with his own. He pushed his tongue inside her mouth, dominating her. There was a dark need that swirled around in his chest. He needed to have her.

Possess her.

Make her his.

He broke the kiss without saying a word and spun her away from him. He pressed a hand between her shoulder blades and guided her to lean on the island. He slid his hand down her spine. He eyed her plump ass and groaned. It was round and begged for him to take her there, but not now.

"Spread your legs, baby."

She immediately did as he'd requested. He nudged the head of his cock at her drenched opening. The heat of her core greeted him. He reached up and took her wrists in his hands and brought them behind her, holding them in place.

"Oh God. Jaxon," Sofie whimpered.

He moved carefully, sliding up inside her. Their

simultaneous moans filled the air. He paused once he was fully submerged in her wet heat. He tightened his grip on her wrist and thrust. It had been too long since he'd been inside her. There was a desperation inside him that he was unfamiliar with.

Her moans fueled him on.

He moved faster, holding her in place while he fucked her.

Her pussy welcomed him, coated him, surrounded him. Jaxon grunted, feeling primal in the taking of his woman.

Because that was what she was.

His woman.

His cock went deeper. Her voice was growing hoarse while she pleaded for more. His movements became faster, harder.

He craved move of Sofie.

And have her he would.

A tremor fluttered through his body. He released one of her wrists, his hand skimming up her back, her neck, and into her dark hair. He gripped it tight and continued to pound inside her.

Sofie's body responded to him. She cried out, shaking, her second climax overtaking her. It was his name spilling from her lips as she reached her orgasm. He shuddered, her muscles clamping down on his cock. She milked him, sending him spiraling out of control.

His orgasm hit him. He continued pumping his hips, filling her with all that he had. Finally, he grew still. He pulled Sofie's body up from the island, still lodged within her. He held her in his arms, kissing the side of her neck, holding her and never wanting to let her go.

# Chapter Twelve

Sofie left her patient's room and glanced down at her watch. It had been a long grueling shift and was finally coming to an end. Her unit was short, as always, and she'd gotten the call yesterday asking if she could come in. She had only agreed to eight hours. She had plans tonight.

Plans that included a six-foot-two, gray-eyed man who took her breath away with one look. Jaxon had left her home yesterday morning with the promise of taking her out, and that would be tonight.

She arrived at the nursing station to see who

would be taking over her patients. She searched for the assignment clipboard but didn't see it. She walked over to where the charge nurse sat and found Chris hunched over it.

"Are you done with the assignment?" she asked.

Joe glanced up from what he was reading and over at her. He was an older guy who had been a nurse for a long time. He was a hard-ass but good at what he did.

"You sure you don't want to stay?" he asked.

"I'm certain." She pulled out her pen and papers from her scrub pocket so she could write down who would be replacing her. There was going to be no convincing her to stay today. Any other day, she would have just picked up the full twelve hours to help out.

"It's really going to hurt with you leaving. Everyone is going to have to pick up someone." Joe took his glasses off and dropped them down on his desk. He gave a weary sigh and stared at her.

"I told Helen when she called me that I can only do eight. This was my off day." She reached for the clipboard and began writing down the names of the nurses who would be picking up her patients.

"But what about being a team. Each nurse will now have to have six patients." He snorted.

"Excuse me?" She lifted her head and glared at him. She always picked up when they called and never complained. She was one of the most senior nurses on their unit and was even charged with training new hires, acting as a resource for others and went out of her way to make sure the unit ran as smoothly as possible. "I know you just didn't try to insinuate I'm not a team player."

"You know what I mean, Sofie. Don't go getting mad. We're all stressed and working short."

"It's not my fault that we are short and it's not my problem." She slammed the clipboard back down and walked away from the desk before she said something that would lead her to be called into the manager's office.

Thoughts of Alana's offer came to mind. Maybe it was time for her to leave bedside nursing. There was so much more she could be doing. Working with Alana would give her some freedom, and she wouldn't have the stress of having someone's life in her hands or the stress of feeling guilty like it was her fault there was a nursing shortage.

She'd have to speak with Alana. Maybe she'd take her out for lunch and hear her friend's offer.

Alana wouldn't lead her wrong, and it would be nice to not have to work such long days.

Sofie breathed a sigh of relief. There was no sorrow in the thought of leaving this job as she thought there would be. She'd miss some of her coworkers, but they could always meet up outside of work.

Sofie finished up her shift and hurried out of the hospital. She slid into her car and leaned back in her seat. She didn't want the stress of her job to follow her home. It was a beautiful day out, and she wanted to enjoy it. Turning on her car, she rolled the windows down to get some fresh air. Throwing her car in drive, she inhaled deeply, breathing in the wonderful air of freedom.

The conversation with Joe pissed her off. No matter how many hours she worked, it was never good enough. She tightened her grip on the steering wheel.

Yes, she would speak with Alana.

But for now, she had planned to get ready for her date with Jaxon. She had the next few days off. That was one perk of working as a nurse. She was only required to work three twelve-hour shifts which was considered full-time. Her extra shifts gave her overtime. Not that her pay was the best. Most people assumed nurses got paid the big bucks, but that wasn't true. For all they had to deal with, the pay was nowhere where it should be.

Excitement filled her at the thought of going out with Jaxon. She didn't know what he had planned. He had been quiet about where he was taking her and what they were doing.

The drive to her home wasn't long. She made it there in record time. She ran into the house and headed straight for the shower. She had to get the hospital smell off of her. In the shower, she scrubbed every inch of herself until her skin was almost raw. Once done, she cut the water off and reached for her towel. She dried herself and stepped out of the shower and went to her closet to try to decide on an outfit.

Not knowing where they were going made it difficult for her. With the weather playing in her favor, she couldn't go wrong with a cute dress and sandals.

"But which dress?" she muttered. Eyeing her closet that was stuffed to the brim, she could admit she might have a shopping problem. She loved trudging through the racks and aisles at her favorite discount stores to find deals. She shoved a few items to the side, trying to decide on what to wear. She finally opted for a white sleeveless shorts jumper that she could dress up. The material was silky, and she had some gold accessories that she could pair nicely with it.

She placed the outfit on her bed, then caught sight of her cellphone on the nightstand with a message. It was from Jaxon.

*Hope you don't mind, I'll be there in twenty.*

"Are you shitting me?" she shrieked. She was still wrapped up in her towel and had to be ready in that short time. She sent back a quick response.

*I can't wait to see you.*

If he wanted to get her early, fine. The hard part of picking out an outfit was done. She tossed her phone back on the nightstand.

"I can be ready in fifteen minutes," she said. She would definitely challenge herself to be ready before he got here. If he arrived and she was still in a towel, they would not be going anywhere. An unladylike snort erupted from her.

He would take it as an invitation to throw her down on the bed and have his way with her.

Not that she would mind.

"Get dressed, Sofie." She chuckled. Grabbing her favorite cocoa butter moisturizer, she sat on the bed and applied it to her entire body. It helped keep her skin smooth and supple.

Fifteen minutes later, clothes on, her makeup and hair was done. Sofie moved to stand in front of her full-length mirror and checked herself out. She had curled her hair loosely where it brushed her shoulders, and her skin practically glowed against the white material of her outfit. She chose a bulky gold necklace that rested right above her cleavage, and it matched the bracelet and her watch.

She snagged her purse from the chair in the corner and slid her feet into her wedge sandals that gave her a little more height. Jaxon would still tower over her, which made her core clench.

"Down, girl," she whispered. Everything about Jaxon made her body tingle. From his intense gaze when he looked at her, to his callused hands as they ran along her skin, to the way his body felt when he was on top of her.

The doorbell sounded.

The man was on time.

After one more glance in the mirror, she headed toward the front door. Butterflies fluttered in her stomach as she approached it. She peeked out the glass window and found Jaxon standing on her porch, taking in her street.

"Hey," she said softly, opening the door.

He turned around, and his quick intake of breath confirmed she had chosen the correct outfit. She stepped out and closed the door behind her. Those butterflies were pounding their wings against her inner walls at the way his eyes lit up when they landed on her.

"Wow," he murmured.

His gaze slid along her as that of a lover's caress. Her nipples tightened into tight buds, growing sensitive as they always did when he was around her. Jaxon stepped toward her and gathered her in his arms. He lowered his head and took her lips in a soft, gentle kiss. Sofie melted against him, her hands coming to rest on his forearms. The kiss was short-lived but packed one hell of a punch.

"You look amazing." He lifted his head and stared down at her. He reached up, running the tip of his fingers down the side of her face.

"You don't look too bad yourself." She chuckled.

Jaxon could wear a paper bag taped around his waist and he would be the hottest man alive. He wore a deep-gray, twill, one-pocket, long-sleeved button-down shirt, with the sleeves rolled up. The top button was left undone, her eyes gravitating towards that patch of skin that was visible. It was the one spot she loved sniffing to catch a hint of his cologne. His dark jeans and black boots gave the allure of a confident male.

"Now where are we going?" she asked.

"Make sure your house is locked up." He motioned to her door.

She rolled her eyes but turned around and ensured her door was locked. She pulled out her cellphone and opened the mobile app to her alarm system. They walked to his car. He opened the passenger door for her and assisted her inside.

A small smile appeared on her lips as she watched him shut the door and walk around to his side. Once her alarm was engaged, she closed the app and threw her phone into her purse. Excitement filled her.

Where the hell were they going?

Jaxon slid into the driver's seat. He started the engine and backed out of her driveway.

"Um, hello? Where are we going?" Her voice ended on a shriek. She giggled at the desperate tone in her voice. She tried not to fidget. She didn't do well with surprises.

"Calm down. You are going to love it." He grinned at her. He reached out and turned on the radio. Old-school rock blasted from the speakers. He sent her a wink. "Sit back and relax."

She playfully scowled at him but did as she was told. The supple leather seats of his expensive car held her captive. The aroma of the leather and Jaxon's cologne wafted around her. She bit her lip and leaned back, watching him maneuver the streets. Once he was on the freeway, her curiosity was piqued.

"How was your day at work?" he asked.

"Ugh, I don't want to talk about it. Let's just say they were not grateful that I even picked up the eight hours. They wanted me to stay longer." She shook her head and wanted to block the day from her mind.

"Okay, I see we need to change the subject," he murmured. Jaxon's warm hand settled on her bare knee. He gave it a squeeze. "You won't have to think about them at all for the next few days."

"Ain't that the truth," she muttered. Cleveland General Hospital would be the farthest from her mind. Sofie's hand settled on top of Jaxon's. She took it and entwined their fingers together. She had a hunky man giving her all of his attention, that was all she needed. "What have you been doing all day?"

"Lots of meetings. Since I'm not in LA, I had to call in to the meetings virtually to discuss some of the options that our agents needed to be able to offer a few new clients they are pursuing. Then some of my personal clients' contracts are up for renegotiating."

"Sounds like you had a busy day, but yet here you are, picking me up earlier than you said. Are you sure you can take off work now?" Her other hand came to rest on top of his. She would have understood if he would have needed to reschedule their meeting.

"Well, that's the thing about being your own boss. You can work when you want, how long you want, from wherever you want to," he replied smoothly.

"I'm certainly jealous." She laughed. Yes, this was making her think of Alana's offer even more. No grueling twelve-hour shifts on her feet having to pull, push, and argue with patients. No getting yelled at by physicians or family members. Working for a consulting firm was looking quite good.

"I heard Alana was trying to recruit you." Jaxon gave her hand a squeeze.

"I'm seriously thinking about it after the week I've had. I used to have so much fun being a nurse, but lately, all of the joy is gone. I don't look forward to going into the hospital anymore," she admitted. A sigh slipped from her. She turned away from him and studied the scenery as it flew by. She took notice of where they were, and she was still confused on where they were going.

"I'm sure whatever decision you make will be best for you."

That was something she needed to hear. She hadn't spoken with anyone else about her unhappiness at work besides Alana. She hadn't even discussed possibly leaving bedside nursing with her parents yet. Her parents had worked so hard to help her get through nursing school, she'd hate for them to think she'd be throwing away all of her hard work. Even though she would still be relying on her nursing degree and her experience if she accepted Alana's proposition.

"How did you get in the business with your brother?" she asked.

"I was his first client." Jaxon chuckled.

"Really?"

"Yeah, right out of college I got drafted into the professional league. I went first round, and London was able to negotiate one hell of a deal for me. At that time he acted as my manager and agent. My third year I busted my damn knee, and there went my professional ball-playing career."

"Oh no." Sofie was listening to Jaxon's story. He shared with her the amount of surgeries he'd had and that his knee had never recovered. After a year of surgeries and rehab, he'd finally decided to hang up his glove.

"But it's okay. I had always known I would be joining London at Primetime, just didn't think it was going to be so soon. As my mother says, everything happens for a reason."

"Your mother is a smart woman."

"That she is, and look at us now. I was able to use my insight of being an athlete to connect with clients, and it helped that I used to play. Many players appreciate someone who has once been in their shoes. Especially the rookies. I can help make sure they are not going to get shitty contracts and deals."

He shared with her stories of some of his clients, good and bad. Sofie listened and watched how animated he was when discussing his job. He loved it. There was no doubt about it.

Jaxon guided the car off the freeway, and it was then she noticed where they were going. She sat up higher and released his hand. She gasped, seeing they were at the airport.

"Jaxon! Where are you taking me?" She turned back to him, waiting for him to answer. The airport. She hadn't even packed a bag. He drove past the parking garages and through the main part of the airport. They entered the private jet field, and it was then she saw the familiar Primetime Sports Management jet sitting waiting.

He parked the car near the hanger and killed the engine. He tossed her a wink and slipped from the car. She sat stunned that they were really about to hop and jet and fly off somewhere.

Jaxon opened her door and held out his hand.

"You are something else," she murmured. Her smaller hand was engulfed by his larger one. He pulled her out of the car and shut the door behind her. "You're just going to leave your car here?"

"They'll take care of it." He dropped a kiss on her lips and entwined their fingers together. He led her toward the airplane.

Excitement raced through her.

Where was he taking her?

"Mr. Keith." A young man dressed in a dark uniform arrived at their side.

Jaxon tossed him the keys to his car. "Hey, Sam.

Park it in the usual spot. I'll be back in a few days."
He slapped the kid on the back.

A few days? Sofie had to hold back the grin
that threatened to erupt. Here she was, being
swept away by a fine, rich man to only God knew
where.

Could the day get any better?

"Yes, sir. I'll even have it washed." Sam smiled
and raced off toward the vehicle.

"He's a good kid." Jaxon laughed. He tightened
his grip on Sofie's hand and brought her closer
to him.

"Can you tell me where we are going now?" she
asked. They were almost at the jet, and she took in
the two people waiting at the stairs to the plane.
The stewardess and one of the pilots.

Jaxon stopped, drawing her in front of him. He
reached up and cupped her cheek. He leaned down
and pressed a hard kiss to her lips.

"I wanted to kill two birds with one stone.
You've never been to LA, so I'm going to take you
there and we'll play tourist, but I do have to admit
there are a few things I have to do at the office
tomorrow."

"LA? But I don't have any clothes. You didn't
tell me to pack a spend-a-night bag?" she cried out.

She only had the clothes on her back and nothing else.

He laughed and brought her flush to him. "Don't worry. A part of being a tourist in LA is going shopping. I got you." He covered her mouth to silence her protest.

# Chapter Thirteen

Jaxon laughed at the excitement on Sofie's face. It was refreshing to be with someone who enjoyed life. Their plane ride from Cleveland to Los Angeles was smooth. They had enjoyed delicious snacks and wine during the trip. He had made reservations at an exclusive restaurant that he couldn't wait to take her to.

They were currently on their way to his home located in Brentwood, California. It was close enough to LA but far enough away where he could have a nice home. The neighborhood was quiet and located on a hillside that gave him premier property and privacy. The neighborhood was ideal for those with families with a great school system and bordering areas with upscale shopping and dining. He'd purchased the home a few years ago and had fallen in love with it.

It also didn't hurt that some of his neighbors were sports and Hollywood celebrities. That meant he got invited to exclusive parties.

"Well, since you have whisked me away for a few days, what do you have in mind?" Sofie asked.

Jaxon had made plans for them, but just he wanted to check on his home and show it off to Sofie. He grew nervous wondering what she would think of it. He wasn't sure why, but he wanted her to love it as much as he did. He had always envisioned starting a family, having kids run through the halls, and sitting out on the balcony enjoying a nice bottle of wine with his beautiful wife.

He glanced over at Sofie and smiled. The car he had arranged to pick them up from the airport was almost to his house.

"Don't worry. You are going to love where we are going out for dinner."

"Food. Good, I'm starving," Sofie said, patting her stomach. She sat up straighter and stared out the window.

The winding hills came into view along with the luxury homes and mansions. The view was the first thing that had attracted him to the area. It was worth every penny.

"Wow! This place is gorgeous. You live in this neighborhood?"

"I do. You see that house over there? That's Kate Landers' home." He gestured to a beautiful multimillion-dollar home that belonged to a well-known actress. Her movies brought in billions of dollars, and she had plenty of awards to her name.

"Are you serious? I love Kate." Sofie pressed her face to the glass. She danced around in her seat. "Her movie, *One Lucky Shot*, is one of my favorites."

"Maybe I can take you over there one day. Her husband and I golf once in a while."

"What?" Sofie practically screamed. Her eyes grew wide as saucers. Their chauffeur let out a chuckle at her bouncing up and down. "Oh my goodness. Please, I'd love to meet her, but I wouldn't want to seem stalkerish."

"Sure. They're good people." He pointed out other celebrities' homes they passed while Sofie still pressed her nose against the window. He had to laugh. It was good to see someone with a natural reaction. Most women he hung around with were only with him for the money and lifestyle he could provide. With Sofie, he didn't have to worry about why she was with him.

"Jaxon, this is amazing. No wonder your mom brags about you all the time." She chuckled.

"When do you talk with my mother?" He playfully pulled her to his side. They would be arriving at his home any moment, but he still needed to touch her. It pleased him to feel her lean into him.

"Almost every time she comes to visit, me and Alana include her in our lunch or shopping outings."

"That I didn't know," he murmured. How had he not known Sofie had been hanging with his mother? He guessed he needed to pay more attention to what was going on.

The driver turned into his driveway. Jaxon's gaze landed on Sofie as they drove up to the house. His breath caught in his throat while watching her reaction to the sight of his home. He couldn't explain why this was so important to him, but it was. "Welcome to my home."

His lips brushed her temple. Her quick intake of breath had his heart fluttering. She gripped his hand in hers.

"This is beautiful, Jaxon," she gasped.

The driver parked the vehicle in front of the three-car garage.

She turned to him with a wide grin. "You better give me a tour."

"Anything you want."

The driver exited the vehicle and opened the door for them. Jaxon stepped from the car first before assisting Sofie out who had focused her attention back on the house. Jaxon took care of tipping their chauffeur while Sofie made her way to the front door. He grabbed his small duffle bag and made his way to her. He took out his keys and opened the door.

"Jaxon," she whispered, taking her first step inside.

He followed behind her, closing the door. They entered his grand foyer with its vaulted ceiling, stone flooring, tasteful artwork on the wall, and a winding staircase that led to the second floor. He tossed his keys in the bowl on the table by the door and tried to see his home through her eyes.

"Come. I'll give you a grand tour, then I need to make a few calls before we leave." He set his bag on the bottom stair then took her by the hand and led her though the home. He took great pride in his house, and it warmed his heart that she loved it.

From the kitchen to the family room and game room, they made their way upstairs where the master bedroom and three other bedrooms were located.

He didn't own the largest house in the neighborhood, but it was a good-sized place to start a family.

"These rooms are so spacious," Sofie noted. They stepped out of one of the guest rooms. She sidled up to him with a playful glint in her eye. "Which one is yours?"

"That one." Jaxon pointed to the last room down the hall.

Sofie spun around and took off toward it. She opened the double doors that gave the allure of a grand entrance to his private domain, and he followed behind her, chuckling at her excitement. Jaxon paused in the doorway, watching her explore his bedroom. Beyond the double doors was a sitting room with a couch and a large flatscreen mounted on the wall. This allowed him to have private living quarters where he could remain secluded when he had company.

Farther into the area was where his sleeping area was with his king-sized bed, oversized wooden dressers, and dual nightstands positioned on each side of the bed. There were two walk-in closets and an en suite bathroom that was fit for royalty. Off the sleeping area was a set of French doors that led out to the balcony that overlooked his yard and pool, along with the neighborhood.

"This house is way bigger than mine, and you stay here all by yourself?" Sofie turned to him.

He had followed her though the quarters, watching her in his space. He found that he really loved seeing her in his private domain.

"I do," he said.

"I don't know if I could go back home after staying here," she muttered.

She spun away, eying the room. She went back out on his balcony, leaning against the rail. He moved to stand beside her.

She elbowed him playfully. "Not that I don't like my house because I do, but yours is a dream home with all the things I would love to have."

Jaxon couldn't take his eyes off of her. Immediately, he knew what he wanted.

"Move in with me."

"What?" Sofie's voice ended on a shriek, and she turned her wide brown eyes toward him. She stared at him without saying a word. What he was asking may have sounded far-fetched, but he wasn't crazy. They were good together, had similar interests, and even though they used to argue all the time, they now knew why.

It was the attraction between them, and they hadn't known how to address it.

"You heard me," he said. He stepped closer to her and reached for her. His hand came to trace her cheekbones while his other one held her by her waist. "Move in with me."

"Wait." She pushed away from him and took a few steps back. She brushed her hair from her face and turned from him. She rested her forearms on the railing and stared off at the scenery around them. "Jaxon, we are supposed to be getting to know each other. Date—"

"We know each other." He moved and stood behind her.

He rested his hands on either side of her and leaned down, nuzzling the side of her neck. Immediately, her body softened, and she leaned back into him. He bit back a smile. Her mind may be resisting, but her body knew who it wanted.

"You know what I mean," she whispered. Sofie spun around in his arms and stared up at him.

"No, I don't. We've spent a lot of time together since London and Alana got married. You probably know me better than any other woman besides my mother."

"And what I know was that you fucked different women weekly." She straightened to her full height and met his gaze. Her jawline tightened, and she folded her arms in front of her chest, putting room between them. "You like to party hard, drink, smoke. But I—"

"That's not me anymore," he interjected. Jaxon ran a hand over his face. He bit back a curse because he couldn't deny what she'd said. He knew his track record, but he couldn't alter the past.

"So you just changed overnight? You expect me to believe that?"

"Yes, I do, because I haven't slept with a woman, or better yet, looked at a woman since we left Bora Bora." He pressed close to her, trapping her against the railing. He needed to make her see that he wasn't the same man he was before. He saw the bigger picture. He knew that he had been wasting his life away when he should have been looking for his future.

A future that included a woman who was meant for him.

That woman was Sofie.

He would do what he must to make her see that

he was genuine. Even if that meant giving her time to see that he had changed.

"This is just too much, too soon, Jaxon," she whispered.

"Don't shut me out," he murmured. He would use the time he had with her to prove that he meant every word. He wanted her and would do what was necessary to win her over. He was a pro at negotiating and sealing the deal with high-paid athletes.

He could win his woman over.

His woman. Those two words sent a flutter of excitement through him. It sounded damn good.

"Don't make a decision yet." He blew out a deep breath and grinned at her. She wasn't going to know what hit her. He'd wine and dine her and show her that she was all that he needed. His past wasn't going to direct his future. "Come. I promised you dinner and fun, and that's what we are going to do."

---

"Jaxon, this is way too much," Sofie scoffed. The amount of bags in the back of his car was ridiculous. As promised, he had taken her shopping since she had arrived with only the clothes on her back.

"What are you talking about?" He slammed the trunk of his truck shut and turned to her. He offered her a sexy grin and pulled her close to him. "Isn't it everything you need?"

"I would have been fine with a few pairs of leggings and t-shirts. You didn't have to go overboard. That is basically an entire new wardrobe, and why do I need suits if I'm only here for two more days?" She laughed. She stepped back away from him to put a little space between them. He'd dragged her from store to store, and before she knew it, there was no room in the back of the truck. She paused and glared at him, resting her hands on her hips. "Don't go trying to win me over with all of this."

"Do you really think I would try to bribe you?" He chuckled. He took her hand and led her around to the passenger door. He opened it, waiting for her to get in.

Sofie eyed him, standing tall, refusing to fall for his charm.

"Yes, I do." She poked him in the middle of his chest with her finger.

Jaxon had been trying to win her over since he'd

popped the question yesterday. She still couldn't believe he had asked her to move in with him. He'd taken her out to a five-star restaurant last night; they'd gone for a drive around LA at night which was beautiful. Afterwards, they had returned to his home where they had soaked in his oversized jacuzzi tub where they ended up making love before retiring to his bed.

Sofie had to admit it was the best first date she'd ever had. He hadn't brought up moving in again since he'd asked.

"Is it working?" He arched an eyebrow at her, tugging her into his arms. He laid one hell of a kiss on her, then assisted her into his vehicle.

She sat back in the plush leather seat while he jogged around to the driver's side.

"Where are we off to now?" she asked.

"We are going to run to my office for a moment." He guided the car into traffic.

The shopping district he had taken her to was full of luxury shops that she normally wouldn't have frequented. The price tag and totals had blown her away. Sofie felt guilty on the amount he had spent on her.

"I can pay you back," she said.

Jaxon's head flew around in her direction. A scowl was present on his face as she glanced at her.

"No, you won't."

"But you spent a lot of money."

"And it is my money to spend how I choose and on who I choose," he said. He focused back on the road, expertly navigating through the crazy traffic that lay ahead of them. "Mention paying me back for anything and I'm going to turn you over my knee."

"Is that a threat or a promise?"

His lips curled up into his sexy grin. His hand tightened on the steering wheel. Sofie shifted in her seat as the image of what he'd threatened popped up in her mind. She bit her lip and figured she would risk it all.

"I'll make payments to you." She reached over and patted him on his knee.

He caught her hand in his and brought it up to his lips. He pressed a kiss to the back of it.

"Oh, you'll pay for this," he growled.

She giggled and snatched her hand back from him.

"I hope so, Mr. Keith," she murmured playfully.

"Keep testing me." His gray-eyed gaze landed

on her for a moment, and in that short time, the heat in his gaze just about set her panties on fire.

They drove in a comfortable silence while Sofie tried to will her body to calm down. Jaxon's promises had her overheating. She fought to kept from fidgeting. Her core clenched with the image of her bent over his knee with her bare bottom facing the air came to mind.

"What do you need to do at the office?" she asked, breaking the silence. She faced her window and watched the city scenery pass by. The glitz and glam of the city was something else. There were so many women who didn't appear to be natural anymore. They all had some form of work done to their faces and bodies. She was glad she was a woman who was born with good looks and the voluptuous body God had given her.

"I was supposed to be meeting with a client, but it looks like he needs to reschedule since his wife went into labor this morning. We shouldn't be long."

Sofie rested and took in the sights while he navigated the busy roads. The music in the car was light, and she glanced back over at Jaxon. The past twenty-four hours had been amazing. She bit her lip and knew she couldn't base moving across the country on them.

But honestly, it didn't matter where they were, she knew it was Jaxon.

Had she caught feelings for him?

Yes, without a doubt, she had.

"Is there something on my face?" he asked.

She blinked, not having realized she had been caught staring at him. They were stopped at a red light. He focused his gray eyes on her, waiting for her to answer.

"There's nothing wrong with your face," she whispered. She reached out and took his hand in hers, threading their fingers together. Her heart stuttered. Was she seriously going to consider his offer? "Why did you ask me to move in with you?"

Jaxon slowly lifted their joined hands and brought them to his lips. He pressed a kiss to the back of her hand. That crooked grin of his was back.

"Because I want you. You are the only woman who fills my thoughts, and I need you with me."

Her mouth dropped opened in shock. She hadn't thought words like that would ever spill from his lips. A horn beeped behind them. He turned his focus back on the road, but he hadn't released her hand. "It doesn't matter where we stay. I'll build a house in Cleveland for you if that's what I have to do."

"Jaxon, you are crazy," she exclaimed.

"Am I?"

Jaxon held on to Sofie's hand and towed her behind him. He was excited to show her the office and where he worked. They had spent the morning shopping. He normally hated it, but watching Sofie's face light up while she'd tried everything made it worth it. The amount he spent didn't matter. He ignored her protest, she needed clothes. As much as he loved seeing her naked body in his bed and home, he wasn't willing to have anyone else see her that way.

"Do you own the building?" she asked.

They came to stand in front of the private elevator banks for the top floors.

"No. Our agency houses the top floor." The door opened, and he escorted her in.

He kept her close to him, needing to feel her. The elevator ascended smoothly. He leaned against the back wall and brought her flush to him, facing him. Her breasts were crushed between them. Sofie's lips parted as if she knew what he wanted. He cupped her cheek and lowered his head, unable to resist those plump lips.

The second their mouths met, he was a goner. Jaxon couldn't explain any of this. He just knew that what he had spoken back in the car was the truth. He needed her.

Hell, it dawned on him.

He was in love with Sofie.

The AI voice of the elevator announced their arrival. He lifted his head and took in the most beautiful woman in the world. It explained everything. Why he couldn't stop thinking about her. Why no other woman appealed to him. Why he compared other women to Sofie.

*I'm in love with Sofie Carter.*

He had to make her his.

"Looks like we arrived," she murmured, her eyes fluttering open.

"It would appear so." He swooped in and pressed another hard kiss to her lips before taking her by the hand and leading her out. He reached down with his other hand and adjusted himself. His cock was hard and demanding satisfaction. It was going to have to wait.

At least until he'd shown her around the office.

"I'll give you a grand tour. Have you ever been to the offices in Cleveland?" he asked.

Their Cleveland office was smaller than the LA one. They had thoughts of expanding and opening one in Miami but hadn't worked out all of the details yet. As the co-owner, he could work from anywhere. Cleveland, LA or, hell, Alaska if he wanted. Wherever Sofie wanted to be, he was willing to make his home.

"Once or twice with Alana," Sofie replied.

The bustle of the office greeted them. He scanned the area, taking in the rows of cubicles surrounded by the higher-level agents.

"Sandi, did you miss me?" He arrived at the desk of the secretary he and London shared.

She lifted her gaze from her computer, a smile on her face. Sandi had been with them since the beginning. The older woman had a few threads of gray sprinkled through her dark hair. Her blue eyes twinkled when they met his. She glanced to his side, and her eyes went wide.

"Hey, Jaxon. Who do we have here?" She leaned forward, resting her chin on her hand.

Her smile was infectious, and he couldn't help but grin as he introduced Sofie to her.

"Sandi, I want you to meet my girlfriend, Sofie. Sofie, this is Sandi, the best damn secretary a man could ask for."

Sofie smiled and offered a hand to Sandi.

"Girlfriend?" Sandi screeched. She flew from around her desk and rushed to Sofie. She swept her in a tight hug while laughing. "If you managed to tame this one, honey, you deserve a hug."

She was just as bad as his mother. Sandi and his mother spoke quiet often, and Jaxon was pretty certain the two of them had been scheming, trying to come up with a way to get him and his brother hitched.

"What is that supposed to mean?" He snorted.

Sandi waved him off. She sat on the edge of her desk and held Sofie's hands in hers. He shook his head and scanned the area and found a few curious looks thrown their way.

"So tell me, how did you two meet?" Sandi asked.

"I've known him for a minute. London is married to my best friend," Sofie announced.

She glanced over at him, and Jaxon's heart skipped a beat.

"Oh, sweet Alana. Aren't she and London just so adorable together?" Sandi gushed.

"They are."

"Okay, Sandi. Y'all can continue this chat later. I want to show her around a bit. Is there anything pressing that needs my attention?"

"Oh, okay, and no, there isn't." Sandi's smile dropped. She gave Sofie another hug. "Now don't be a stranger. I can tell you plenty of stories about this one here."

"I look forward to hearing about Jaxon." Sofie winked at her.

"Sofie knows me well enough," he muttered. He guided Sofie away amidst their giggles. He held back a smile himself. Sandi would never speak ill of him or his brother. They were like the two nephews she'd never had. "Let me introduce you to the rest of the office."

"Are you serious? They are offering him how much money?" Sofie leaned forward in shock, staring at the computer screen. She was just blown away by what she was learning from Jaxon about his job. She knew that as a sports agent he dealt with a butt-load of money, but she didn't know it was like this.

"One hundred and fifty million dollars for five years," Jaxon replied. He kept his arm around her waist as she sat atop of his lap.

She had a hard time concentrating while he explained how the teams were able to offer up so much money, all the players had to pay, and what they would be left with afterwards.

She hadn't realized how much went into the business of professional sports. She had heard of numbers before that were thrown out on the news when stories broke. But she didn't know what was going on behind the scenes. There were a lot of people involved in these deals, and they all had to be paid.

"Now I see why they go and get endorsement deals to make extra money. I just thought they were being greedy." She chuckled.

"There's nothing wrong with getting paid for your talent." He pressed a kiss to her bare shoulder.

She glanced down at him and took in his steamy gaze. Her core clenched at the desire burning in his eyes.

"Unfortunately," he said, "being able to play for years can take a toll on one's body. So pursuing endorsement deals are smart."

"Do you ever miss it? Being on the other side?" she asked softly.

She couldn't help it. She wanted to feel his hair between her fingers. She lifted a hand and raked them through his thick, dark hair. The strands were soft and parted easily for her. Jaxon blinked and for a moment grew eerily silent. She wasn't sure if he was going to answer the question.

"Sometimes I do. I remember what it was like being on the road, staying in hotels, hearing my name called out from fans. The adrenaline of a win is like nothing I ever experience until…" His voice drifted off.

"Until what?"

"Until I met you," he replied. "My heart races from the moment I know I'm about to see you until you are standing in my arms. There's no better feeling than being able to kiss you and hold you."

"Jaxon, are you trying to make me fall for you?" she whispered. Her heart was racing at the moment. She couldn't believe it, but she felt in her heart that she was. It was too soon.

Wasn't it?

She reached up and cupped his face in her hand. He leaned into her palm, his gray eyes holding hers.

"Please tell me it's working," he whispered.

Sofie had never seen him so vulnerable before. Cocky? Sure. A jokester? All the time.

All of his emotions laid out before her?

She never thought she would see the day.

"Oh, it's working, Mr. Keith." Why was she fighting this? Hadn't she been ready to jump into online dating? Why not jump feet-first into whatever this was with Jaxon?

Sofie was done fighting.

She was head over heels in love with Jaxon Keith. Her stomach grew into knots just thinking of leaving him and going back to Cleveland. He was trying his best to prove that he was no longer the person she had thought he was.

Sofie leaned down and brushed his lips with hers.

"So I need to keep working on it?" he asked. His hands settled on her waist, and he lifted her off his lap and turned her to face him.

She straddled him and wrapped her arms around his neck.

"This is a good start." She chuckled. Her dress rode up, exposing her hips.

His warm hands rested on her thighs.

"I thought you would say that." His lips curled up in the corner.

His hands were definitely a distraction. If his hands slid up higher about three inches, he'd be at the edge of her panties. If only he would slip them and dive underneath her small cotton—

"Well, I'll be damned," a familiar voice appeared behind her.

Sofie's head whipped around to find London and Alana standing at the entrance of Jaxon's office. The couple stood stunned.

London chuckled and wrapped an arm around Alana's shoulders. "When Sandi said Jaxon was showing Sofie around, I didn't think she meant your Sofie."

Sofie froze. Alana stood unmoving next to her husband. The pain brimming in Alana's eyes felt as if someone had taken a knife to Sofie's heart. Alana spun around and dashed out of the room.

"Alana!" Sofie cried out. She pushed off Jaxon and raced after her friend. Guilt tormented her as she hurried behind Alana who stopped by the elevator banks. "Please. Let me explain."

She paused a few feet away from Alana. Her friend kept her back to her. Sofie's heart sank. She had never meant to lie to her or hide anything from her. They had been friends for too long, and this was something she had never done before.

"It was Jaxon back in Bora Bora, wasn't it?" Alana asked. Her voice was low and husky.

Sofie winced internally. This wasn't the spunky bestie she had known and loved. This was the voice of a woman who had been hurt.

"The one you were sneaking around with," Alana added.

"Yes." Sofie wasn't going to lie anymore to her. It was time she came clean. She had planned to share with Alana, but she wanted to make sure what they had was real. Now she wished she would have had the balls to just tell her, no matter what would have happened between her and Jaxon. "I was going to tell you."

"I thought we were friends?" Alana spun around and glared at Sofie. She pushed her glasses up on the bridge of her nose. "When did we start lying and hiding things from each other? Did you think I couldn't handle you dating my brother-in-law?"

"We weren't dating," Sofie said. She immediately regretted it.

Alana narrowed her gaze on her.

"Honestly, we didn't think anything was going to come out of what happened in Bora Bora."

"What about what we talked about the other day? Or was that a lie, too?"

"No, that wasn't a lie. Jaxon and I—I mean I—ended what we had at Bora Bora. I didn't want to be hurt by him, so I chickened out and broke it off. Then I regretted it but was too proud to tell him I'd changed my mind so I was going to try to get over him by dating other guys."

"And you couldn't say any of this before? I'm your best friend. You've been by my side when my parents died, my failed relationships, and stood by my side at my wedding. But something like this, I couldn't know or be a part of?" Tears streamed down Alana's face.

It broke Sofie's heart.

"You couldn't trust me?" Alana said.

Sofie gulped in air, trying to push down the wave of nausea that threatened to overtake her. She wiped away the tears that balanced on the edges of her eyelashes. She loved Alana like a sister, and to see how much she'd hurt her friend, it sent a shooting pain through her.

"Of course I trust you." Sofie took a step toward Alana. She hesitated for a moment and hated that she had put them in this predicament. It all could have been avoided had she been honest from the get-go. "I'm sorry I've been such a lousy friend lately. I promise I didn't mean to hurt you. I didn't want to burden you with my issues."

She arrived in front of Alana and studied her. Alana reached up and wiped the tears from her cheeks.

"That's what friends are for." Alana sniffed.

"Say you'll forgive me?" Sofie moved closer to Alana who grabbed her and wrapped her up in a strong hug. Sofie returned it hard, fighting back her tears.

"Of course I do. How could I stay mad at you?" Alana's hold tightened. She pulled back and studied Sofie. "So what gives? Do you love Jaxon?"

"I do," Sofie responded without hesitation.

"You do?" Jaxon's voice was quite close to her.

It was then she felt him behind her. She released Alana and slowly turned around to face him.

London brushed past them and went over to Alana, gathering her into his arms.

Sofie's heart felt light with her admission. She nodded, unable to speak. Jaxon's arms wrapped around her, bringing her into his warm embrace. She nuzzled her face into the middle of his chest and inhaled.

This was home.

This was where she was supposed to be.

Sofie glanced up and took in Jaxon's killer-watt smile.

"I'm so glad to hear that, because I'm in love with you, too." He caressed the side of her face with his knuckles. A look of wonder appeared in his eyes as he gazed down on her.

Sofie frowned.

She felt funny. She didn't know why, but—

Sofie broke from Jaxon's hold and spun around. She eyed a tall trash can positioned next to the elevator and rushed toward it. She made it just in time for the contents of her stomach to spill from her lips. Her stomach heaved, evicting everything she had eaten earlier that day. She squeezed her eyes shut in embarrassment once her stomach decided to stop. She rested her hands on the edge of the can, and her knees shook.

"Are you okay?" Jaxon rested his hands on her shoulders.

Sofie inhaled sharply then immediately regretted it. The smell of vomit assaulted her. She lifted her head slightly and jerked it into a nod. "I think so."

"What was that?" Alana asked. She stood nearby with a look of concern. "Did you eat something bad?"

"I don't know," Sofie said. She wiped her mouth with the back of her hand. She blinked a few times and straightened to her full height. She breathed in the fresh air that didn't reek of vomit. She wished there was something she could drink to battle the lingering taste in her mouth. "That was weird."

"Let's go back to my office." Jaxon gave her a squeeze.

She took two steps away from the can, then she dashed toward it again. She leaned over it, expelling what was left in her stomach.

Jaxon paced the length of his bedroom with the feeling of hopelessness overtaking him. He had been thrilled to learn that Sofie loved him, but he couldn't celebrate the way he wanted to. He had offered many times for the chance to take her to the hospital.

He paused and glanced over at her.

Sofie leaned back against the pillows on his bed. She opened her eyes and met his gaze.

"I'm okay," she murmured. Her eyes fluttered shut again.

Jaxon didn't know if he believed her or not. He

had brought her to his home last night, skipping their planned dinner. He'd ordered takeout for them, and Sofie's food had been skipped.

Just the scent of food sent her scrambling into the bathroom.

"Sofie, this is not right. Allow me to take you to the hospital. I don't like this," he murmured. He moved toward the edge of the bed near her and took a seat. While they should have been celebrating and planning their life together, something was making her sick.

"I'm sure this is just a little bug and will be gone soon." She reached out and took his hand in hers.

Sofie was one hell of a woman. Here she was, the one ill, but was comforting him instead. He just wanted her back in his arms and well.

"You haven't been able to eat and only had small sips of water," he started, but she cut him off.

"If I don't feel well by tonight, then I will let you take me to the emergency room. I promise," she said.

She offered a weak smile, but Jaxon wasn't buying it.

A knock sounded at his door. He glanced over. Alana burst into the room with London trailing behind her.

"I went to the store and got you a few things," Alana said. She paused at the sight of Jaxon sitting next to Sofie. She grinned sheepishly. "Hey, Jaxon. Sorry to interrupt, but I purchased a few things that should help."

"You are such a good best friend," Sofie murmured. "What would I do without you?"

"We will never know." Alana chuckled. She sat the bags on the foot of the bed and reached inside one of them. "But first before anything, I need you to do this."

She tossed a small box at Sofie. Jaxon leaned over and watched Sofie pick it up. His eyes widened at the item.

A pregnancy test.

"Alana, just like I told Jaxon, it's probably a stomach bug or one of those twenty-four-hour viruses," Sofie said.

"Well, then humor me and take the test," Alana said. She rested her hands on her waist and glared at Sofie as if to dare her to do otherwise. "If it's negative, then I have a bunch of medications I picked up from the pharmacy."

"Fine," Sofie groaned.

Jaxon stood and assisted her to the edge of the bed. His heart was racing.

Could it be?

Anything was possible.

He began to sweat with the possibility that Sofie could be pregnant with his child. He had always wanted a kid or two but had never focused on it, pushing it aside for the future. He had never been with a woman who he could see a future with.

Now he had Sofie.

"You got it?" he asked.

She nodded and paused as she swayed for a moment, getting her bearings. She snagged the test from the bed and slowly made her way to the bathroom. Alana walked alongside her and went in with her, shutting the door behind them.

Jaxon stared at the door in bewilderment.

"You look like it should be you lying in the bed." London chuckled.

Jaxon ignored his brother's attempt at humor.

"What if she is pregnant?" he whispered.

"Then you will man up and take responsibility," London snapped.

"It's not me I'm worried about," he said. Jaxon looked at London, and for the first time in his life, felt unsure of something. He had wanted to build a life with Sofie. The first step had been asking her to move in with him. She still hadn't given him an answer. Now this. What if she didn't want to move in with him? He blew out a deep breath and explained to his brother how he had asked her to move with him.

"What's the rush?" London asked.

"Because I want her with me always." Jaxon blew out an exasperated breath. How could he explain to where his brother would understand?

"If you love her and want her, then wait. She won't go anywhere. Sofie is a smart woman, and anyone can tell how much she loves you. I don't know how I missed it before. The way you two look at each other reminds me of Alana and me." London slid his hands into his pockets and strolled over to the windows and leaned against the windowsill.

Jaxon didn't know when his twin had become so wise.

The door to the bathroom opened with Alana stepping out. She smiled and waved to the door.

"She wants you to wait with her," Alana said.

He jerked is head in a nod and rushed into the room. He found Sofie sitting on the floor in front of the double vanity sink. He shut the door behind him and walked over to her. He slid down next to her.

"Everything okay?" he asked.

Sofie reached out and took his hand. She offered him a smile and squeezed him tight.

"It will be." She sniffed. Her big brown eyes held unshed tears. "No matter what, it will be."

"I know it will be." He lifted her hand and kissed the back of it. "I love you."

Sofie's features softened. She leaned against him with her lips curling up into a smile.

"I love you, too." She pressed a kiss to his lips then rested back against the wall. "I've made up my mind about my job."

"Really? What is that?" he asked.

"I'm going to leave the hospital and sign on with Alana. I think change would be good for me. I'm going to put in my two weeks' notice immediately once I get back home."

"That's awesome, baby." Jaxon knew this had to be a hard decision for her to make. She'd been a nurse for a while, and he could see she wasn't happy besides her telling him she wasn't. He couldn't imagine doing a job he didn't love. He would be miserable.

"And I've made a decision about what you asked me," she said softly.

Jaxon stiffened for a moment. He wasn't sure

which way she was going with this. He inhaled sharply, ready for whatever decision she would make. He already had his argument ready should she say no. He would prove to her why it would be best for them to live together.

"What is that?"

"My answer is yes. I'll move in with you, but only on one condition." She paused.

"And that is?" Jaxon's heartbeat thundered so loudly in his ears he was barely able to hear anything.

"I like LA and all, but it's not really me. Can we keep a house in Cleveland? With me joining Alana as a consultant, it may be best for me to be available there."

"Anything you want." He gathered her to him, lifting her to where she straddled him. Her knees rested alongside him while she wrapped her arms around his neck. "If you wanted a place on the moon, I would have figured it out."

Her laughter was music to his ears. She leaned down and kissed him. Her soft lips sliding along his was enough to awaken a desire in him that always burned for her. He immediately took over the kiss, thrusting his tongue inside her mouth. She whimpered, her fingers diving into his thick hair. He loved how she always tugged on his strands.

"Wait," she panted, pulling back from him. "Have we forgotten already why we are here in the bathroom?"

"Is it time?" he asked.

"I believe so." Sofie pushed up off the floor and walked over to the counter. She picked up the long white test stick and stared down at it.

"What does it say?" Jaxon was impatient and stood from his perch on the floor and joined her. He stared down at the result window, the breath escaping him.

*Pregnant.*

Jaxon ran a trembling hand along his face. He couldn't believe it.

He was going to be a father. Tears appeared in his eyes. He grabbed Sofie and brought her into his arms. They held each other for what seemed to be forever. Jaxon couldn't be happier. He had the love and affection of the woman he loved, and now they were going to be starting their family. His mind was already racing with the things they would need to do and purchase to prepare for the little one. His brother would be able to help with planning, and now Chance would have a cousin to grow up with.

Everything was perfect.

"Are you happy?" she asked. She raised her brown eyes, her tears streaking her face.

"Ecstatic," he murmured. He used his thumb to brush away her tears. She was the most beautiful woman in the world to him and she was having his child. "Have I told you how much I love you?"

"It's been a while, but I'm always open to hearing it again."

*One Year Later*

Sofie hefted her son onto her hip and returned his smile. Karver Keith was five months old today, and he was one of the happiest babies she had ever known. He shared the gray eyes that were known of the Keith men. He was the perfect mixture of her and Jaxon. He had his father's eyes, curly dark hair, a light tan, and had her personality.

"Come now. Your cousin, uncle, and aunt should be here by now." She picked up the dirty diaper and tossed it in the trash in the corner of his room and headed out of his nursery. Her son had a fresh diaper, had just received his after-nap feeding, and should be ready for visitors.

In the past year so much had happened. She had resigned from Cleveland General Hospital. Once she had returned to work and saw that they were still working shorter and the environment just wasn't safe with the ratios they were wanting nurses to work with, it had made her decision even easier. They hadn't wanted to accept her resignation and they'd tried to negotiate with her, but Sofie had made her mind up. It was time for her to move on, and she couldn't be any happier.

She had thought working for her best friend would be awkward, but it was anything but. Alana had been patient in teaching her the ropes of the new company. They were already flourishing and doing well. Some of Alana's old clients had followed her, and with Sofie's intimate knowledge of medical charting, she was able to lend her knowledge. Together, Alana and Sofie worked well as a team.

Sofie made her way down to the first floor of their new home. As promised, Jaxon had built them a new house in the suburbs of Cleveland. They went back and forth from LA to Cleveland due to

Jaxon's job. It was easy now that Karver was an infant. When he got older, they would have to consider which home would be their primary place of residence.

"There's my beautiful wife," Jaxon said.

She breezed into the kitchen and went immediately to his side. He plucked Karver from her arms. Her son squealed and laughed seeing his father. The two of them had a close connection. Jaxon blew raspberries on Karver's neck. Their son laughed and giggled, reaching for his daddy's nose.

"You may want to be careful. I just fed him," Sofie warned.

"Thanks for the heads-up." Jaxon chuckled. He had learned the hard way he shouldn't jostle a well-fed infant close to feeding. Karver had vomited milk on his father's face, shirt, and the floor. That was a day Sofie was certain to remember for a long time. "London just texted me that they are almost here."

"Did you get the grill started?" she asked. She moved over to the fridge and pulled out items she needed to make the side dishes. She placed everything onto the wide island but was trapped in place by her husband.

"I did." He wrapped an arm around her waist

and drew her back to him. He nuzzled the side of her neck.

She sighed, loving the feeling of him against her.

"I missed you, Mrs. Keith."

"You just saw me, Mr. Keith," she replied. She glanced at him, finding him holding her in one arm while Karver was resting on his father's chest in the other. She spun around and pressed herself to him.

They had been married six months ago in a small intimate wedding. Just a few friends and their families. That was all they needed. Sofie had no desire for a lavish wedding. They took their vows in front of God and their close loved ones.

"No, you don't get what I'm saying," he murmured. He lowered his head and pressed a soft kiss to her lips. "I miss you, Mrs. Keith."

He wagged his eyebrows, and then Sofie understood what he was saying. The hard bulge resting on her stomach was an indicator of how much he missed her. She grinned and rubbed herself on him.

"There's nothing we can do at the moment. Alana, London, and Chance would be here any moment," she said.

"My brother would understand if I asked him to man the grill and watch his nephew while I go and speak with my wife privately." Jaxon lowered his head, nuzzling the crook of her neck.

Her knees grew weak. He snuck his tongue out and licked the soft, sensitive skin of her neck. A whimper escaped her. His offer was sounding really good.

"Jaxon," she moaned slightly. She blinked rapidly, trying to not fall for her husband's seduction. Her breasts ached, and it wasn't from being too full of milk.

No, she was getting aroused, and she was tempted.

"Say the word, wife," he growled. He lifted his head and planted another soft kiss on her lips.

The doorbell sounded. Jaxon arched his eyebrow, waiting for her to make her decision. Her core clenched at the heated look in his eyes. She bit her lip and exhaled.

Dammit, she couldn't resist him.

Sex between them was still explosive, and she was still addicted to her husband. During her pregnancy, she couldn't keep her hands off him, and it'd been the same afterwards.

"Thirty minutes." She poked his chest with her finger.

His wide grin spread across his face. He repositioned their son in his arms. Karver was resting his head on his daddy's chest and appeared to have dozed off.

"I only need twenty." Jaxon gripped the back of her head and swooped down and kissed her until her toes curled up. He broke the kiss and winked at her. "Go upstairs, and I'll take care of them."

He gave her bottom a slap, sending a surge of desire through her. She spun around and raced to the stairs and headed up to their bedroom.

There was never a dull moment in the Keith household. Sofie arrived at their master suite and immediately shucked her clothes. She kicked her shorts off, her shirt soon followed. The pile grew until everything was off. She sat on the edge of their bed in all of her naked glory. Her body was practically on fire waiting for her husband to arrive. She didn't have long to wait until the door opened and Jaxon strolled in. He flicked the lock shut.

A pleased glint appeared in his eyes as stalked toward her. Sofie's pulse spiked at the heated look in his eyes. She bit her lip and watched him approach her.

He tugged his shirt over his head and tossed it down. His cargo shorts joined her pile of clothing along with his boxer briefs. He arrived in front of her with his erect cock straining toward her. She glanced down at it and licked her lips. There was a drop of precum on the tip that she ached to lap up.

"Hold that thought," he murmured, tilting her chin up so he could stare into her eyes. Her husband could always tell what she was thinking. He lifted her and placed her on the middle of the bed. "There will be plenty of time for you to suck my cock, baby. Right now, I need to taste you."

"Jaxon," she whimpered.

He pushed her down onto her back. His warm hands slid down her thighs and rested on her knees. "Open those legs, Mrs. Keith."

She did as she was commanded and was soon rewarded with his talented tongue sliding through her slickness. A moan escaped her, and she knew he was going to make good on their thirty minutes. Without a doubt, he was going to wring one hell of a orgasm from her and him.

Sofie dove her fingers into Jaxon's thick locks and held on for the ride.

# A Note From the Author

Dear reader,

I'm so glad that so many of you asked for Jaxon and Sofie's story. I hadn't intended to write another story in this world, but I'm grateful that you reached out to me. This one was so much fun to write and it was nice being able to bring London and Alana along for the ride.

I hope you enjoyed Mr. Arrogant. Please don't forget to leave a review on whichever platform you purchased this book.

love,

Peyton Banks

# About the Author

*USA TODAY* best selling author, Peyton Banks is the alter ego of a city girl who is a romantic at heart. Her mornings consist of coffee and daydreaming up the next steamy romance book ideas. She loves spinning romantic tales of hot alpha males and the women they love. Make sure you check her out!

Sign up for Peyton's Newsletter to find out the latest releases, giveaways and news! Click HERE to sign up or visit her website www.peytonbanks.com!

Want to know the latest about Peyton Banks? Follow her online:

Dirty Justice (Special Weapons & Tactics 5)

Dirty Trust (Special Weapons & Tactics 6)

Dirty Secrets (Special Weapons & Tactics 7)

Dirty Ultimatum (Special Weapons & Tactics 8)

<u>Trust & Honor Series (BWWM)</u>

Dallas

Dalton

<u>Interracial Romances (BWWM)</u>

Pieces of Me

Hard Love

Retain Me

Silent Deception

The Christmas Secret

<u>African American Romance</u>

Breaking The Rules

<u>Mafia Romance Series</u>

Unexpected Allies (The Tokhan Bratva 1)

Unexpected Chaos (The Tokhan Bratva 2) TBD

Unexpected Hero (The Tokhan Bratva 3) TBD